CADE'S C

Sam Cade had struck it rich. He was the happiest man alive as he led his gold-burdened mules in the direction of home. Then out of the morning sunlight came a bullet that was aimed for his heart. Out of the saddle he toppled but, thanks to some Aztec magic, he didn't die.

Ralph Figgins and his daughter Henrietta fished Cade out of Ute Canyon. Cade found them friendly people, and he promised to visit them; but that was something which would have to wait, for his gold was gone, and he didn't take kindly to thieves and killers....

CADE'S GOLD

by
Bill Wade

MAGNA PRINT BOOKS
Long Preston, North Yorkshire,
England.

Wade, Bill
  Cade's Gold

  ISBN 1-85057-328-X

First Published in Great Britain by Robert Hale Ltd, 1987.

Copyright ℗ 1987 by Bill Wade.

Published in Large Print 1988 by arrangement with Robert Hale
Ltd, London.

Printed and bound in Great Britain by
Redwood Burn Limited, Trowbridge, Wiltshire.

CHAPTER ONE

Sam Cade knew that his face wore a self-satisfied grin. He could not help it, for he had succeeded at last, and a man in his position had the right to feel pleased with himself. Folk had been telling him all his adult life that he would never do it. They had called him a no-account idler and wastrel. But he had known different; and now he was going to make his critics back in Hazewater eat their words. For those three mules strung out behind his horse were carrying several hundred pounds of ore that was as near pure gold as most people were ever likely to see. Only a fire assay could provide the final verdict, of course, but he reckoned that he was carrying home the kind of fortune that would keep him in fair style for the rest of his days. Yes, sir! He had done it! The rear right-hand corner of that cave back on Warbow Creek—producer of no better than a few modest nuggets to begin with—had turned out to be a mass of almost solid gold when he had cut away the masking rock.

Letting his horse make its own pace, Sam inhaled deeply and looked up and around, taking in the raw beauty of the Stillwater Ridge to the south of him and the plunging gulf of Ute Canyon on his immediate right. The air tasted good, and colours were bright, with the new green of late Spring in evidence where vegetation grew in gleaming rags and tatters up and down the edges of this arid place, and the vivid orange flame and royal purples of the cactus flowers peeped out of shadows that were darkened by the flaring sunlight. Altogether, it was a joy, for up here a man could taste the richest wine of life; while to sober him— if he needed it—the primeval silence of the ages known only to God came swelling off the mountains and reminded him of his mortality. Oh, but Sam was happy and fulfilled! This Nevada wilderness, which had for so long been an enemy and the source of his labours, had become his friend. He had his youth, he had his health, and now he had riches too. He had everything!

But then he had nothing; for there was a tremendous blow in the middle of his chest and he passed from light into darkness in a particle of time that could not be measured by the instruments of Man. The bang of the rifle did not register in his ear, and there was not even the fleeting awareness that he had been shot—much less any consciousness of falling from his saddle. He could have been dead, and stayed dead for ever, and that would have been all there was to the story of Sam Cade.

Yet he wasn't dead. Though when he became dimly conscious of himself again, he perceived that all the workings of his body were paralysed and that he possessed only a blind awareness of what was happening to him. The condition was totally unlike any experience that he had ever had before, and inexplicable in any terms which he had heard used to describe a normal form of semi-consciousness; but he knew that he was not alone for he could somehow detect the presence of two men standing near him. They were talking in what reached him as a strangely grating monotone and, though it was possible to understand them, the sound put recognition out of the question. He had the notion that he knew at least one of the pair, but that was as far as it went.

He heard the first speaker say: 'Ain't this a master piece o' luck. There's a fortune ridin' on them three mules.'

And the second voice answered: 'Yeah. It's ours. We keep our mouths closed about this job. Okay?'

'Why, sure. It was our idea. Nobody else

9

thought of it for us.'

'Glad we agree.'

'When didn't we?'

Laughter rasped briefly, music of the devil's fiddle.

Then the first speaker went on: 'We must get rid of the body. I see diggin' tools on the first mule.'

But the second voice said: 'Damned if I fancy diggin' a grave in this heat. 'Sides, scoop the top soil off about here and you hit rock.'

'Hell—sure. We'll toss him into Ute Canyon. I've heard the water's real deep down there.'

'What about his horse?'

'Shoot it.'

'Seems best.' Then the first speaker had a sudden change of heart. 'No—no. Let it wander back to town. Natural-like, d' you see? Folk will figure he had an accident up here, and soon forget about it.'

'Better a mite o' speculation,' the second voice agreed. 'Folk are too sure they know when somebody lights on a shot horse.'

'Let's pick him up, then, and cast him over the brink yonder.'

'Is he dead? He don't look dead.'

'They never do this soon. Great day! You plugged him straight through the heart. Look at all that blood.'

10

'Yeah. It was a good shot. But—'

'Stow it!' the first speaker advised impatiently. 'He'll be double dead when he reaches the bottom of the canyon. Get hold of his feet. Lift—and carry!'

At that moment the paralysis that gripped Sam's body began to ease. He felt something of the hands that held him, and also the sensation of being carried—though nothing of being cast into space—but once more felt a little as a mass of jutting foliage checked his plunge, and there was even a short, flashing vision of the tough growth bending under his weight and then folding downwards to the extent that it rolled him into a new stage of the fall into which he had been so callously hurled.

Then his fleeting glimpse of the canyon wall rushing past him was again lost in darkness. Once more there were moments in which he could have been a dead thing. But then he revived for another splinter of time as he struck water and the chill of immersion seemed to galvanise his stunned nerves. Now he felt himself sinking deeper and deeper into the cold liquid and, his sight returning in full, watched bands of light and shadow wobble out of symmetry and become part of the murk which boiled up like foul smoke as his feebly threshing form touched the bed of the river.

11

He hung against the bottom. The instinct to survive jolted him through his senses as a blurting panic. In a split second his mind despatched its inspectors to question in every corner of his body. Their reports came in and assembled at a lightning rate. It seemed that, apart from the blow to his chest, he was unharmed in any way, and even the damage to his chest was now dissipating. Without being aware of it, he must have filled his lungs at the moment of entering the river, for he found that he was holding his breath and seemed in no immediate danger of drowning. It was the presence of the current that worried him so much, for it appeared as if there were some vaguely intelligent force that was sliding across the top of his body and holding him down. According to the movements of his arms and legs, he ought to be rising towards the surface by this time, but in fact he remained spreadeagled on the bed of the river and had just started bumping along with its westward flow, seemingly unable to find either the strength or the wit to overcome this smothering presence.

Then he realized that he was rising, though not in response to his own efforts, for the water was becoming steadily shallower and he was literally floating upwards into the light with the planing action of the same current that had been threatening to drown him not quarter of a minute ago; and shortly after that the river lost all traction on his frame and he bobbed back into the air, spitting and spluttering, and stones rattled beneath his knees as he first jack-knifed with the flow and then began dog-paddling for the safety that he sensed could not be far away; and almost at once he found that he was crawling rather than swimming where the river ran only inches deep through a central channel that had sandbanks on either side of it which extended like bright yellow wings towards the next stretch of deep, fast-flowing water about two hundred yards ahead.

Sam eased himself slowly to his feet. Stones ground treacherously under his soles and threatened to upset him, but he managed to part his legs and settle his stance, then he wiped the water out of his eyes and began inhaling the clean canyon air. After that, his body replenished with oxygen, he turned back his head and gazed upwards between the soaring walls of rock that enclosed him, asking himself how in hell he was going to get back to those places above where the sun shone down with all its fierce heat and the blue of the sky seemed so close that you could reach up and touch it.

He was trapped. There was no other word that would meet the case. He had by a miracle survived this far, but those two damned thieves might still have done for him. If he attempted climbing out of the canyon—up either wall—he was going to fall and break his neck. He had no doubt about that, for he had never been much of a hand at scaling rock and had no head for heights. Okay. There was still the river, but he wasn't much of a swimmer either, and he knew that down stream of him—between this spot and the three mile distant safety at canyon's end—were several stretches of swift flowing rapids, where spurs of jagged stone thrust out of the depths and tore the surface into cruel races and whirlpools of drowning foam. Once let the river pick him up in those conditions and he would not stand a chance. The erratic forces of the flow would soon drive him under, and that would mean a lonely funeral for whatever part of him was found on a mountain shoreline one of these days.

Thus it would be sheer madness to try saving himself by wading off down river. So what about attempting it in the opposite direction? To his certain knowledge the waters flowed more gently east of here. But once more there was a snag; and it was a big one. For about half a mile back from this place—round the left-hand bend that he could see in the canyon as he faced about—the river emerged from a tunnel, after flowing a quarter of a mile underground, and he had no idea at all of what the subterranean course was like. The waters might flow shallow, under a roof that arched high above them, or they might flow deep and meet a low roof for much of the distance through the tunnel. His problem was at best perplexing, and at worst daunting; but, all in all, he calculated that his most likely salvation lay back there. He'd do well to treat it as a gamble. That would take the sting out of the risks he ran. For he had always been a man who enjoyed a gamble. Even when the odds were clearly against him—as they were here.

He started moving against the flow, and in a few moments was on the edge of a deep water again. Stepping up to his thighs in liquid, he felt the stones of the bottom roll under him and claim his balance. He slid instantly out of his depth and began wallowing. Bracing himself, he attempted to kick out into a swimming stroke, but the current met him at once and he lacked the skill to make his strength count against it. The waters seized him and spun him like a top, driving him back in the direction from which he had come, and again he climbed back coughing and choking into the shallows, knowing that, from the weakness of his

15

performance against the slight obstacle which he had just tackled, he could forget progressing beyond the spot that he was already at.

Dripping and shivering, he pushed himself erect again and stood there like numchance. What in heaven's name was he to do? He was indeed the prisoner of Ute Canyon. True, he was in no immediate danger, but he could not stand on the river-bed indefinitely. The temperature above the walls of the canyon was fit to fry eggs, but down here—standing in waters which the sunlight could not reach—he was going to slowly freeze into immobility if he didn't do something constructive. But what?'

Getting more and more chilled and unnerved, Sam splashed back and forth through the shallows for another hour or so; then, giving way to something that was akin to panic, he began to shout for help. He found relief in this, though he realized that the chance of there being anybody in the neighbourhood to hear him was one in tens of thousands—for this high western part of Nevada was about as remote as you could get—yet, for all that he expected no answer, an answer did come, and he stopped his bawling through cupped hands in mid-word, convinced that some devil straight out of the hot place was riding the echoes and taking the juice out of him.

'Hello, there!' came the hoarse and distracted reply of a man's voice from above. 'Where are you?'

'Down here, g'dammit!' Sam returned in his mightiest bellow, the canyon rolling 'dammits' about him from then to evermore.

'Where?'

'Down here!'

'Hey?'

'You deaf?' Sam demanded enormously. 'That's if you are there, mister, and I ain't plumb crazy!'

'I'm here,' came the jaundiced response. 'But you may be plumb crazy! Wouldn't wonder in fact— holdin' court in that hole!'

Miracle of miracles! There *was* somebody up there on the rim of the canyon's northern wall. Sam could see a man peering in his general direction, apparently without seeing him and, despite the awful tugging of his damaged chest muscles, lifted both arms above his head and waved them frantically.

Then he made out the much higher pitched shouting of a woman's voice and realized that there was also a female on the rim. She was moving slowly back and forth and gazing fixedly down. 'I can see him, pa!' she announced. 'He's standing in the river—right beneath

17

where I am now! Can't you see?'

'I can see him!' the man answered irritably. 'How in Pete's name did you get down there, boy?'

'Get me up!' Sam almost stamped. 'Get me up!'

'Don't see how,' the man observed reasonably.

'Ropes!' Sam advised. 'Haven't you got ropes with you?'

'Why, sure,' the man replied. 'Me an' my daughter got ropes—but they ain't long enough. It's a fair way down to you, boy.'

'It surely is!' Sam agreed ironically. 'I fell it. See how far your ropes will hang down! There ought to be a horse o' mine somewhere near you. I carry a rope on the saddle, cowboy fashion. Put that with yours!'

'All right,' the man above shouted back doubtfully. 'We'll do what we can.'

'And then some!' the woman added, sounding far more confident about it and bucking Sam up no end. 'I can see your horse yonder!'

The pair withdrew from against the sky, and Sam went on gazing upwards at the space from which they had vanished. Filled with impatience and apprehension, he had to discipline himself not to start shouting again and, by the time ten or fifteen minutes had gone by without any further developments on the canyon's rim, he had gained a nasty crick in his neck. But soon after that his would-be rescuers reappeared and the man dropped a large coil of rope towards him from a point on his right beneath which the wall of the canyon was almost vertical and none too generous with its hand and footholds, though there was also an absence of vegetation down that part of the cliff and it was the avoidance of this kind of obstruction to the lifeline that the man on the edge above had clearly had in mind. Unhappily, though—despite the other's latest forethought—he had been right in the first place about the length of the ropes. They were now fully unwound down the rockface, but their lower end was swinging back and forth above the river and at least fifty feet beyond the reach of Sam's upraised hands.

Moving until he stood directly beneath the lifeline, Sam studied his difficulty with a calculating eye. It was all up to him now; his helpers had done what they could. Somehow he had got to reach the rope. That meant he'd got to climb. He must ignore his lack of ability, and get on with it. But not while still wearing his boots. They must come off, for they were sodden through, and his feet felt like lumps of pudding inside them.

Sitting down in the shallows, he pulled his boots off; then, slackening the belt that held up his trousers, passed the tops of the boots under the encircling leather and then drew the buckle tight again, fitting the footwear securely into the bend of his groins. The arrangement was not a comfortable one, but he didn't believe that it would impede his attempt to climb and, rising again, he stepped right up to the bottom of the rockface and sorted out the initial holds for his fingers and now naked toes.

Lifting himself onto the cliff, he hung with his arms bent and his legs at full stretch; then, forgetting the fears that plagued him, he crabbed and scrambled upwards, his view of the rope's end never leaving his eye, and knowing instinctively that to freeze at this juncture would be fatal to his further efforts and bring about a fall into the waters below that would shame him and perhaps cause his potential rescuers to give up in disgust and leave him here to die.

Hardening his resolve, Sam increased his efforts and inched his way upwards, muscles bunched and sweat dribbling down his temples. there was a price to be paid for every yard that he gained, and he broke his fingernails back into the quick and skinned the tip of his nose while checking a heart-stopping slip. It was in many respects the test of a lifetime, and desperation was his final goad, but he fought his vertical path from one tiny knob or ledge to the next and, nearing exhaustion—despite the relative shortness of his ascent—he at last reached the rope and gripped it tightly, only too conscious now that, even with its aid, he could never reach the top of the canyon wall without some kind of further help, for the muscles of his feet and hands were beginning to cramp and he would simply not be able to hang on through the ever intensifying demands that the rest of the climb would make on him. But then he heard the woman's voice again. 'Hold tight, mister!' she called down. 'We've attached the top end of the rope to pa's saddle. His horse will pull you up!'

'Let her rip!' Sam shouted back. 'I'll stick like glue to a blanket!'

The pull began. With the rope wound about his hands, Sam found himself moving upwards at a steady rate. Holding fast proved less easy than he had suggested it would be, but he was still gripping the lifeline as the pulling animal hoisted him over the rim itself and then dragged him a short distance across the dusty ground beyond. Now, recognising that he was safe, Sam released his hold on the just stationary rope and, shutting his eyes to the sun's glare,

21

stretched out flat upon his back. It was wonderful just to lie there and relax, and the fact that he hurt all over was the most marvellous proof that he was still alive.

He heard the approach of running feet. A figure came between him and the sun, creating a dark image behind his eyelids, and he was aware of being scrutinised and then stirred by a shoe on the underside of his right thigh. 'Are you dead?' the female voice asked.

Sam opened his eyes, enjoying what he saw, for she wasn't more than twenty, had a beautiful face, and the kind of shape to her that you wouldn't find more than once or twice in the whole of Nevada. 'Do I look dead?'

'Yes, you do.'

'Well, if that ain't a caution!' Sam protested. 'There's me, a thunderin' fine figure of a man and a holy terror among the bustles—as they'll tell you from Carson City to Reno—and she tells me I look dead.'

'What nonsense are you running on, Harry?' demanded the male voice which had been last heard by Sam when he was at the bottom of Ute Canyon; and the man himself came striding in from the spot where he had just left the horse that had been used to hoist the trapped Cade out of the gulf.

'I was only telling him he looked dead, pa,'

the girl explained clapping her floppy hat a bit tighter on her blonde hair. 'Looks to me like somebody shot him through the heart. See for yourself.'

'To hell with that!' Sam snorted, sitting up. 'I promise I ain't more than slightly dead. Rely on a woman to stir it. Can't a self-respectin' ghost catch a minute's rest these days?'

CHAPTER TWO

Sam considered the man now. He was a big guy, over six feet and slightly run to seed, with shaggy grey hair where the bronze of his pate didn't show through, rough-cut features, and a faintly warlike aura. 'I give you good morning, sir,' Sam said.

The big man squinted southwards. 'As to that, it could be afternoon.'

'Whatever,' Sam acknowledged. 'I'm mighty obliged.'

'You're mighty lucky.'

Shifting his gaze, Sam grinned at the girl. 'Must be my day.'

The blonde knew what he meant. 'Hush now!' she ordered, blushing. 'Ghost? A girl could feel scared around you at that.'

'Nicely scared?' Sam hoped.

'I'm her father,' the big man warned. 'I've kicked butts on her account. Don't you give him any encouragement, Harry. I've seen his like before. He's halfway to a bad lot. I can tell.'

'You're an accurate judge, sir,' Sam allowed. 'I know folk not so far from here who'd tell you I'm the whole way bad. But you've got me greatly interested. What's that Harry stuff? Your girl don't look like no Harry to me.'

'I've been his only son these twenty years,' the girl hastened in. 'It happened when I was ordered. There was a mix up at the baker's.'

'Now Henrietta,' her father complained, 'You must not mock your papa.'

'I see,' Sam commented. 'Henry—Harry. Yeah.'

'You tryin' to be smart, Mr—?'

'Wouldn't know how to be,' Sam assured the other disarmingly. 'The name's Cade. Sam Cade, of Hazewater, when at home. Which ain't all that often.'

'Ralph Figgins,' the big man responded, digging a thumb into his chest as if there were some chance that he had not introduced himself plainly enough. 'Me an' my daughter have just come back from Hazewater. We went in and paid the sheriff a call.'

'Did you now?' Sam mused. 'I reckon I ought to call on the guy myself. You didn't happen to see two men with three heavily laden mules as you came in this direction?'

'No,' Figgins said; and his daughter shook her head.

'Um,' Sam rumbled. 'Maybe the hellions went Warbow Creek way.'

'I take it they did you some harm,' Figgins said.

'You take it right,' Sam replied.

Figgins glanced towards the canyon, then asked: 'What'd they do?'

'Shot me and threw me down there,' Sam rasped, telling his rescuers the rest of what had happened to him in the fewest words that he could summon.

'By Hector!' Figgins mused. 'All that gold! Warbow Creek, you say? Harry and me have been grubbin' over in Lode Valley—where we're just headed back—these six months, and all we had to show for it was that bag o' nuggets that got stole out of our tent while we was at work.' He rubbed his nose, snuffling. 'I found the tracks left by two men after the theft. Ain't too much to suppose it was that pair robbed you too.'

'Probably the same men,' Sam conceded. 'You told the sheriff about them?'

'I spoke of two men, Cade,' Figgins said. 'What more could I say? I ain't the first notion of what they look like. How about you? Did you get a look at their faces? Anything?'

'No, Mr Figgins,' Sam answered seriously. 'Like I told you, I was riding along—minding

26

my own business and in love with the world—
when bang; and I was as near dead as I'm going
to be until I die for real.'

'How in tarnation *did* you survive that
bullet?' Figgins demanded, shaking his head
over the pierced and stained condition of Sam's
shirtfront.

'We're both miners,' Sam explained, 'and
you know as well as me that a miner needs his
luck when he's digging for gold. Now, sir,
there's nothing like a gold charm for luck, and
when I took up the trade I figured I ought to
have a real ripsnorter of the kind. So happens
I know an old Mex-Indian down in Sonora. I
paid this old guy a visit—and told him of my
wish to get taken suddenly rich—and he dug
into his great-great-grandad's Aztec chest and
fished out this fiery sun medallion, which is two
and a half inches in diameter and a half inch
thick. My old friend give it me—because I'd
done him an important service once—and he
told me that it'd bring me all the gold I could
carry and protect me in life and limb. All I
mustn't do was sell it, lose it, or give it away.'
Now Sam put a hand into the front of his shirt
and drew out the Aztec charm, revealing that
it had an eye at its top through which was
threaded the cord by which the disc was
suspended from his neck; and then he showed

the father and daughter where, at the centre of the charm—in fact dead in the middle of its fiery sun emblem—a lump of lead was embedded to the extent that its tip had actually pierced the medallion through and broken the flesh of its victim's chest, thus bringing about the copious bleeding which had caused his would be killers to take him for dead. 'So there you are, Mr Figgins,' Sam ended, dropping the medallion back down the front of his shirt. 'I don't swear there's anything to Aztec medicine —or any other kind of native medicine if it comes to that—but I can't deny that my old Mex-Indian friend got it right somehow. That gold charm found me gold, and it also stopped the bullet that would have killed me. I'm not going to sell it, lose it, or give it away. Though I'll maybe take it back to Sonora one of these days for repair.'

'Trouble is,' Figgins reflected, 'your charm may have done what it was supposed to do— but you're no better off now, are you?'

'Not just now,' Sam admitted. 'Could the sheriff tell you anything about them two robbers—always allowing yours and mine were the same, of course?'

'Not a thing, Cade. If you ask me, that damned sheriff is not interested in much but gettin' through an easy day.'

'That sounds like the Jack Stockman I know too,' Sam acknowledged. 'So far as I'm concerned, he's neither use nor ornament, but Hazewater elected him, and that's that.' He grimaced thoughtfully. 'Does Stockman aim to do anything for you?'

'Said he'd ride his rounds and keep his orbs liftin'.'

'That's just what I figured,' Sam growled, his voice expressing resignation but echoing not a trace of the anger that he felt deep down. 'How are you fixed, sir?'

'For what, Cade?'

'Cash money,' Sam answered, smiling to turn aside the offence that he feared Figgins might be about to take. 'People have got to eat. I've still got a few dollars more than I should need—'

'No—no,' Figgins said, his right hand making a dismissive gesture. 'Me and Harry hold. There's some game at the back of Lode Valley, and she can shoot a rifle as straight as most. Me, I can stand jackrabbit with a mite o' seasoning, and I wouldn't ask better than venison at Saint Peter's table. Hell if I would, Cade! Me and Harry can live off the land, and if this here theft has set us back some, you may be sure the gold will come again. The Good Lord has always met our needs—just about.'

'Seems to me,' Sam said, 'we can't rely on the law for much. If there's to be help in our trouble, it will have to come from Samuel Cade and Ralph Figgins.'

'You proposin' something?' Figgins inquired narrowly.

'What's it sound like?' Sam responded.

'No, boy,' Figgins said, glancing towards his daughter. 'I've got responsibilities that you haven't got. 'Sides, I'm getting too old to go gallivantin' around the countryside vigilante style. If you'll be ruled by me, you won't say much and you'll keep your nose out. Angry sheriffs and fleein' outlaws come about the same. I know you've lost plenty, but what's gold beside your health and strength?'

'A lot of work done,' Sam gritted, 'and a lot of fun lost. But I ain't a fool, Figgins. In one way you're right—good and right—but in another you're wrong. Sometimes these things even up, but not always. Like you say, though, you've got your responsibilities, and every man must please himself.'

'Don't you use me as an excuse for any thing, pa,' the blonde Henrietta cautioned. 'Mr Cade's right. You can't throw it all away.'

'He's as he is,' Figgins said shortly.

'I figure him for rough-and-ready,' the girl

retorted—'but honest, brave, and strong—and right.'

'And on the sunny side o' thirty,' Figgins sniffed. 'A woman at the diggings is one thing, but a female vigilante is another. That critter we can do without.'

'He said it, Mr Cade,' the girl observed drearily. 'I'm female.'

'I had arrived at that conclusion myself,' Sam said dryly. 'He's your papa, Harry, and I reckon he knows what's best for you both. Us mining folk ain't much good at entering into agreements anyhow.' Grinning, he lurched to his feet, pulling the boots out of his belt and then letting them fall at his feet. After that he made a perfunctory effort to squeeze some of the riverwater out of his garments, then walked to a nearby rock, boots in hand and, seating himself again, dragged and kicked the footwear onto his feet, his eyes seldom off his rescuers as he did so. 'With your permission, Mr Figgins, I'll pay you a visit in Lode Valley before long.'

'We'll be glad to see you,' the blonde Harry assured him.

'Ain't sure myself but what we oughta move over to Warbow Creek,' Figins remarked. 'All that gold you say you took out of the place.'

'You must suit yourself, sir,' Sam replied.

'This here is a free country. But I've dug over Warbow from end to end, and I do promise there's no more gold in the rock. You might pan out a certain amount of what them geologist folk call residual dust, but the gold was one strike, and I made it.'

'Passing thought,' Figgins said indifferently. 'If Warbow's plumb gutted, I'm confident there's still gold in Lode Valley.' Giving his substantial midriff a pat, he belched. 'Damn beans! Fetch them ropes of ours, Harry; and our horses too.' He watched the girl move to obey, face expressionless. 'You goin' to be all right, Cade?'

'You bet,' Sam said. 'No lasting harm done. I'll last for fifty or sixty years yet.'

'Say you don't know, boy,' Figgins advised. 'There may be another bullet waiting for you. That Aztec medallion covers a mighty small part of your hide, and I don't figure it's a lot more good now. The lead it stopped most likely let the medicine out.'

'You don't have to be wrong,' Sam admitted, watching uncritically as Figgins' daughter separated two *riatas* from the rope which had been used to pull him out of Ute Canyon, coiled them with quick hands, and restored them to the saddles of the horses which belonged to her father and herself. Then she returned to

Sam's lariat, and coiled that too, and was about to go and catch his horse—which was standing to the north of them and not all that far away—when Sam called: 'Drop the rope on the ground, Harry! I'll do for myself! And thank you!'

'Pleasure,' the girl responded, carrying the lasso to him for all that and putting it into his hands. 'Those boots don't look all that comfortable.'

Standing up once more, Sam tried to wriggle his toes in the shrinking leather. 'They ain't,' he said.

'We'll leave him to his misery, girl,' Figgins chuckled, offering his hand. 'You'll be welcome if you do ride over to Lode Valley.'

'Thanks,' Sam said, meeting the other's strong grip and shaking. 'You two saved my life. I'm in your debt. I'll try not to forget it.'

'Fare-you-well anyhow,' Figgins said, nodding; and then he put a hand on his daughter's left shoulder and steered her towards her horse.

'Goodbye,' the blonde said, craning.

' 'Bye, Henrietta.'

The girl smiled and, if her papa resented the familiarity, he didn't show it, for he was smiling to himself as he turned away from her and walked to his horse. Then the pair stepped up, the blonde moving with a long-legged freedom in her levis, and gigged their mounts into a trot, the dust rising behind them as they headed westwards.

Sam gazed after them, but they soon grew small upon the face of the surrounding land; and then, moving out to his left, he caught his horse and hooked his lariat back on the saddle; and after that, his thoughts still somewhat with the girl and her father—and very much with the pain and deep emotions of the experiences which had preceded their appearance—he mounted up himself and angled back towards the canyon, pursuing the trail that ran close to its edge for about sixty yards eastwards and then halting beside the rock-pile on his right from which he believed that the ambush shot fired by one of the two men who had robbed him must have come; for he was determined that he was going to begin an investigation of some kind before he left the area.

He walked to the rear of the heap of boulders. Here he found an oblong of sand with a tangle of buckthorn and greasewood backing up to the canyon's edge. He studied the sand, for it was a loose carpet, and in its surface were visible the numerous impressions made by a couple of horses and those also cut by two pairs of high-heeled riding boots.

Crouching, Sam studied the footmarks first—certain from their unsmudged freshness that they could only have been left by the robbers—but they told him no more than that the boots involved were in both cases of average size and in a good state of repair. Thus, accepting that an average sized boot usually went with a man of like build, he must look after this for two men of medium physique, which meant that he would have to take into account about sixty or seventy percent of the male population when seeking for the pair who had shot and robbed him. He sniffed ironically. Where did that conclusion get him? The answer was—nowhere.

Sam shifted his attention to the hoofprints, though he was already predisposed to believe that he would be wasting his time even more surely here than he had with the footmarks, and this made the movement of his eyes rather quick and careless. He could well have missed what was there to be seen in the mass if he had not come upon an isolated shoemark which had a look of distortion about it. Bending closer, he soon perceived that the slight crookedness of the impression was no illusion and that it could be seen at several other spots also. He pondered the matter—not that any special brains or imagination were required—and arrived at the judgment that one of the horses brought to this place had been wearing a loose, worn shoe that had moved on its nails each time the animal had lifted the affected hoof and set it down again, with the result that the initial impression made by the metal spread to the left or right as the mount's full weight came to bear. Now this *was* of some use, though it did not help in any immediate sense—and might not help at all, since a change of shoes would promptly eliminate whatever evidence could be deduced from the sign here. No, it was very likely one of those things that promised only to deceive, and might even mean that he was getting too clever for his own good.

He straightened up, the palm of his left hand putting a little pressure on the Aztec medallion which had saved his life and the area of bloody bruising behind it. Then he glanced to his right and upwards, absorbing the obvious steps of the climb by which the top of the rock-pile could be reached; and, though he did not feel much like making the effort, he raised himself onto the lower stones and then ascended the zig zag course which carried him upwards for about twenty feet and brought him to a position of vantage from which he could look down along the trail over which he had just ridden up and imagine how easy it had been for the ambusher to sight on him dead centre and squeeze off. Next he looked among the summit boulders—and then those in the next layer down—for any trace of the cartridge case used in his bush-whacking, but the would-be killer had either not bothered about ejecting the fired shell after his murder attempt or had pocketed it at once like the careful assassin that he had every need to be.

Sam descended the rock-pile, then walked back to his horse. Standing beside the creature, he patted a saddlebag with the back of his right hand. In there, holstered on his gunbelt, he kept his Colt forty-four. He was tempted to get the weapon out and buckle it on, since the men who had tried to kill him might still be around or spot him in Hazewater, should they journey to that town—as well they might to call in at the Assay Office with a specimen of his ore—but, despite the fact that he would be offering the unknowns every advantage by walking unarmed, he did not wish to call special attention to himself today by entering Hazewater with his pistol strapped to his waist. He had always played the man of peace in town and, as nearly as possible, wished to pass unnoticed for the time being, since he could not forget the distorted dialogue which had reached his befogged mind after the bullet had struck him. The talk had undoubtedly suggested that the two thieves worked for a boss, yet liked to do a little for themselves on the side; so it was probable—in fact almost certain—that they would put his gold into a hiding place, perhaps not too far away. What he must bear in mind was that should he do anything that brought on public trouble with the two thieves, he could arouse the interest of their boss—which might result in an interrogation of the robbers by that man—and that could mean more parties entering the doings and his chances of recovering his gold being reduced accordingly. He must tread carefully and hope for a lot of luck. Since it would be impossible to conceal the fact that he was still alive and no amount of care would help much if events went against him.

Again he mounted up. The sun beat down on him as he kneed his horse into motion, and his shadow thrust back off his left shoulder. He rode straight ahead, and Ute Canyon left him on the right about thirty minutes later. Then, at the end of an hour, the trail turned left and away from the mountains, entering a steep fall through arid rocklands that eventually merged with the more fertile country towards the Carson Sink. Down there, over to the east and three miles away, was the town of Hazewater, which was already visible in terms of a church spire, some false fronts, a few red-tiled roofs and the clusters of trees at its further end.

Sam covered the better part of another two

miles, and realized that entering town was in prospect within the next quarter of an hour. He glanced down at himself. His chest had been bleeding again, but appeared to have stopped now. He appreciated that he could not ride into Hazewater looking like a fugitive from the shambles and decided that he had better change his shirt. There was a clean one in the saddlebag behind his left knee. It would be as well to stop here and put it on.

He brought his horse to a halt. Then he swung down and unbuckled the saddlebag. He took out his clean shirt and spread it on his saddle, then he stripped to the waist and threw away as beyond redemption the garment which he had just removed. Dipping his chin, he examined himself to make sure that his injury had indeed finished leaking, then pulled on his replacement shirt. After that he looked himself over with a far more critical eye than usual, since, despite the heat of the day, he was still not quite dry from the soaking that he had received in the river and his levis had picked up enough dust to appear filthy. He would have liked to change his trousers also, but he couldn't—because he hadn't got another pair— so he would just have to ignore that part of his condition and hope that his appearance would not give too much offence to the more fastidious members of Hazewater's upper crust, who had been exhorting the common folk to toilet and dress-consciousness during the last year. Not that Sam gave half a damn about the slickest of them anyway. It was just that he did not wish to be noticed.

He buckled up his saddlebag again; then, as he was preparing to remount, a metal object that was lying at the middle of the trail and a few yards beyond his horse caught his gaze. He peered hard, shading his eyes. The object look-ed like a horseshoe. Though that did not make it a particularly unusual sight, for horses the West over were constantly casting hoof-irons. It was simply that there were bright new scrat-ches on the shoe lying there which suggested that it had been thrown quite recently—within the last hour or two in fact, knowing how quickly metal oxidised in this atmosphere—and that, stirring up his memory of the horse with the loose shoe that had stood behind the rock-pile off which he had been shot at, made the sight a thousand times more significant than it would normally have been.

Leaving his horse, Sam walked to where the cast horseshoe lay and, picking it up, turned it over and over in his hands, seeing that it had a well-worn toe, punch-holes that were more fancy than the common run, and a couple of bent nails still clinging to it. Frowning, he considered his find with complete objectivity. Could this possibly be the loose hoof-iron from the horse belonging to one or the other of the two men who had tried to murder him? If he were to base any action on this object between his hands, he must first be reasonably sure about it. But the fact was, when everything was taken into consideration—like the time element, how seldom this high trail was travelled, and the position of Hazewater as the only substantial town for miles around—it was almost bound to be. A man could become the complete doubter and, when that happened, he could waste his life from the continuous failure to believe. Well, he wasn't going to let that happen here, and he returned to his horse and slipped the hoof-iron under the flap of his saddlebag, knowing exactly what he was going to do with it when he reached town.

The crimes that had been committed against him might not prove so difficult to solve after all. Judging from the cast horseshoe's advanced state of wear, the owner of the horse that had thrown it might be having a new set fitted to his mount at this very moment. The answer to everything could be found at Gerry Stubb's forge.

CHAPTER THREE

Shortly after that, with the clock on the church tower showing the time to be two-fifteen p.m., Sam rode into the western end of Hazewater's main street. The day was still at its most scorching, and he saw very few people actually walking around in the sun. There were, of course, loafers in the shadows, and he sensed that he was a source of interest here and there, but neither a hand was raised in greeting nor a word spoken, and it seemed to him that he could hear the dried out timbers cracking in many of the frame buildings on either side and see the fleas hopping off the old dog scratching on the midwife's doorstep.

Sam passed a hand across his brow. He wasn't feeling too sharp again. The place seemed airless and everything was out of drawing. He spat unashamedly as the familiar stink of horse excretions fouled his mouth and nostrils, and he was tempted to ride on and take a siesta in the trees about the small lake hidden at the end of the way—as he had done a few times before—but the purpose was still strong in him, and he kept going only to the centre of the main and the blacksmith's shop, where he dismounted and tied his horse at a hitching rail.

Taking his time about it, he removed the worn horseshoe from his saddlebag and then walked in at the open front of the smithy, his thoughts on how best to tackle Gerry Stubbs, the giant blacksmith, with his business, for it had delicate aspects to it, and he feared that Stubbs—a short-tempered man, who took himself and his work a mite too seriously—might decline to become involved if he once fully understood what his visitor had in mind; so the trick, then, must be to handle matters as obliquely as possible, without bringing actual deception into play.

Waves of heat immersing him as he approached the sooty brickwork of the forge, Sam saw Stubbs, half-naked within a buff apron, labouring at his anvil. The sparks were flying about the smith as his hammer rose and fell on the strip of red hot iron from which he had just started fashioning a horseshoe, undoubtedly for the buckskin mount that stood on the earthen floor next to the stone dais that supported the blacksmith's fire-bed, chimney, and bellows.

Speaking no word yet, Sam looked around him, bent on finding out before he did anything else whether or not the buckskin's owner was in the building, but he and Stubbs seemed to be the only human beings present; so, as he could now see that all four of the buckskin's hooves had been stripped off and rasped level, he decided to go as far as he could without asking any form of permission and picked up a worn hoof-iron that he imagined had recently been stripped from the horse waiting to be re-shod, holding it beside the shoe that he had found on the trail to the west of town and making the best comparison he could; but it needed no expert eye to see that the two horse-shoes had originally belonged to the same set, for the gauge of the metal was similar and the punchwork and nails identical. It seemed to Sam there could be no serious doubt that the buckskin was the horse which had cast the shoe that he had picked up on the trail and that, by the same token, its master must be one of the two men who had attempted to kill him and then stolen his gold.

'What's the game, Cade?' Gerry Stubbs suddenly asked, his dark face scowling as he paused in his work to make his visitor aware that he had missed nothing. 'You're like an old ferret nosing around. What's your business in here? Have you got a horse you want shod? Something you want mended?'

'Take it easy, Gerry,' Sam soothed. 'I don't want any work done, but I would like to know who owns that buckskin over there.'

'Why?'

'Seems to me I know it from someplace,' Sam lied sweetly. 'Got a notion I may owe its owner a mess of sow-bellies.'

'When were you ever in such a hurry to pay a debt?'

'Did I ever keep you waiting, Gerry?'

'I guess you didn't,' the blacksmith admitted ungraciously. 'What were you doing with them irons? Looked to me like you was comparin' 'em.'

'Sure. I picked up the first one near the door. Little things please little minds. Right?'

'Right.'

'What's his name, Gerry?'

'Don't know it, Cade. The man's fairly new around. I've seen him a few times—on the street and in the stores—but we've yet to have any talk socially. He's got a Jewish look. If you want to know all about him, you'll have to ask Charlie Anstey.'

'My cousin Charlie?'

'He's your cousin Charlie's pal.'

'Well, I never!'

'It's what comes of living out in the gold-fields,' Stubbs observed disdainfully. 'The

45

world goes whizzin' on, and you miss it all by grubbin' in the dirt and gettin' nowhere.'

'Y'know, Gerry,' Sam said judiciously, 'I must be missing somethin'. It must be a heap more interesting to be a blacksmith than I'd supposed. Or maybe it's the place. What settlement is this?'

'Cade,' Stubbs said, giving the hot iron on his anvil a terrific whack and allowing his hammer to vibrate for a moment or so, 'you're sassing me.'

'Wouldn't dare, Gerry.'

'Got rich yet?'

'I'm working on it.'

'In here you're not.'

'You're doing it all,' Sam pointed out. 'I'm due for a week off anyhow. Maybe two.' Chuckling, he raised his hands, as if to protect himself. 'Don't say it, Gerry. You might hurt my feelings. You know how tender they are.'

'You've got a hide like a bull buffalo!' the smith contradicted. 'Get out of here! You're asking for the toe of my boot!'

'Just going, Gerry,' Sam said, his voice much harder and far more businesslike. 'You don't have to suffer me, and that's a fact. How long is it since that buckskin was brought in for shoeing?'

'Half an hour—give or take.'

'By Charlie Anstey and his Jewish pal?'

'Who else?'

'Must be sure,' Sam said defensively, knowing full well that things which sounded as if they must be often weren't. 'Where'd they go when they left you?'

'Dunno,' Stubbs replied. 'The horse was left with me. When I've finished shoeing it, I'm to stand it outside. They'll be back to fetch it, and pay me. But there was no time given for anything.' He dipped the newly shaped hoof-iron into water, and steam hissed into the atmosphere. 'There, nosey, you've got it all! Are you satisfied?'

'Yes, I am,' Sam answered brazenly. 'Thank you, and good day.'

'You cheeky—!' the blacksmith began, cutting himself off abruptly and shaking his head. 'Well, I guess all the town knows what you are.'

Shrugging resignedly, Sam let Stubbs have the last word, and then he stepped out onto the street, returning to his horse. Gripping the animal near the mouth, he fetched it round in the middle of the way and walked it back in the direction from which they had lately come, turning it into a side opening on the right when they had covered about forty yards and leading it down the lane which they had entered until they came to a cottage property on the left that was bordered by a rough hedge with a wooden gate set at its centre. Stopping outside the gate and tying his horse to the rail adjacent, he entered the cottage grounds and began following a path towards the front door of the dwelling itself; but he was still several paces short of the entrance when it opened up and a well-shaped but rather horsey-faced girl with thin, russet-coloured hair, small, probing eyes of grey, and a proud, petulant air, stepped out and headed towards him, smiling a welcome. Sam stopped instantly, grinning a mite warily in reply, for this was cousin Lucinda Anstey, a good enough girl in her way, but one who was unable to forget that she had once got him into bed when they were younger and had figured that that gave her certain rights in perpetuity where he was concerned. One of these days he'd take a bride, but for all the damage that Lucinda claimed he'd done her—and she had so happily let him do her— that bride would not be Miss Anstey. No sir! 'Hello, Lucinda,' he greeted.

'Why, hello, Sam,' she simpered 'To what do we owe the honour?'

'Charlie around?' Sam inquired. 'I know he's in town.'

'He was here,' the girl responded. 'But

he's gone off again.'

'With that friend of his?'

'Issy Kaufmann, yes.'

'Where've they gone?'

'That I couldn't rightly say,' Lucinda answered. 'But it seemed urgent. They said they were in a hurry. Issy borrowed my horse.'

'Does he often do that?'

'Never done it before. His'n threw a shoe out on the trail. Him and Charlie left the critter with Gerry Stubbs.'

Sam avoided comment. 'Did you see which way they went?'

'What is this?' Lucinda pouted. 'I don't see you above two or three times a year these days, and now you waste a visit asking questions about my brother—and that Issy.'

'I want,' Sam began, suddenly reflecting that he wanted nothing of the sort, for he hadn't really thought out this stage of the business properly up to now, 'to speak with them.'

'You'll have to wait for that,' Lucinda said. 'Those boys went off at a fair lick.'

'Which way?'

The girl frowned; then, sighing, jerked a thumb over her left shoulder. 'That way.'

'Northwest,' Sam observed, blinking. 'What would they want over there?'

'Do you care, Sammy?' she wheedled, giving

him that conspiratorial leer of hers that always meant one thing. 'I've something you'd much rather see. Bought 'em from a New York store. Sent all the way back East for 'em.'

'Like what?' Sam asked absently, his mind still chasing cousin Charlie and this Issy Kaufmann character.

'Frilly drawers. The latest fashion. Real red silk and they're open at the legs.'

'They sound mighty fetchin',' Sam admitted.

'Come on in. I'll show them to you.'

'That'd be nice,' Sam said, even more absently. 'I'd like to come in, but I haven't got time.'

'Haven't got time!' Lucinda exploded angrily. 'What do you mean—you haven't got time? If you aren't at work, you've got plenty of time!'

'No offence!' Sam hastened. 'No offence! Think of what your ma and pa would say if they caught you showing me things like that.'

'They're out,' the girl said. 'Visitin'. We can have the house to ourselves.'

'Sounds good,' Sam conceded. 'Real fine. But I've got to ride after that pair.'

'You won't catch them up, Sam.'

'Maybe not, Lucinda,' he allowed, still puzzling as to where cousin Charlie and Issy Kaufmann might have hidden his gold—if they

50

were guilty of his attempted murder and the robbery, as they very well could be, since Charlie was no good and had been aware for months that Sam was digging with a certain amount of success out at Warbow Creek. He tried to concentrate through the girl's watchful annoyance. The hiding place would have to be somewhere to the southwest of town, for the time element of the crimes and the geography of the district insisted on it, but the two could hardly be going back to the cache now and must be involved in some quite different business—unless their riding to the northwest was a blind and they meant to swing back in the Ute Creek direction once they were well clear of Hazewater. He didn't know. His mind was full of possibilities; but he was sure of nothing. He could only obey instinct; and instinct said that he was to follow his cousin and Issy Kaufmann and find out what they were presently about. 'Must go, Lucinda, I may not catch 'em up, but I'll sure as hell give it a try.'

'Beast!' Lucinda slapped his left arm, and growled deep in her throat. 'You've been lying with one of them old girls at the cathouse!'

'You're dead wrong,' Sam said wryly. 'I can't afford 'em.'

'You don't have to afford me.'

'Another time,' he said firmly—real firmly.

51

Then he turned away from her and walked back towards the gate.

'You—you,' Lucinda faltered behind him. 'I'll get even with you for that, Cousin Sam. You see if I don't!'

Sam lifted a hand in farewell, but didn't look round. He felt a trifle guilty as he stepped out into the lane and freed his horse. Women! They seemed to think that men lived only for them. He could hope that Lucinda had at last learned otherwise.

Stepping up, he set his horse moving towards the end of the short lane on which uncle Bert Anstay's cottage stood. Clearing the rough growth that bordered the brief way, he passed into an area of bunch-grass—where a few cows were cropping, their tails on the swish—and he suddenly found himself wishing that, for all his sentiments of a minute ago, he had not put Lucinda's back up quite so thoroughly. He knew she was as vengeful as she was contrary and, if she said she'd be even with him, this way or that she would. Perhaps he should have told her a little more, but she *was* cousin Charlie's sister, and there was no telling what might have come out of it if he had started saying things that could be dressed up as accusations. Anyway, he couldn't worry about her for now. His job was to find whatever sign had

been left by Charlie Anstey and Issy Kaufmann, then ride after the two men as fast as
he could.

The grass soon petered to a close, and beyond
it lay ribbons of shale and broken rock. Here
the tracks left by cousin Charlie and Kaufmann
were instantly visible. Riding parallel with the
sign, he was soon sure that the pair travelling
ahead of him had had no intention of swinging back towards Ute Canyon once beyond
town, for their tracks never deviated by more
than the width of a rock-pile and formed a vir-
tual beeline towards the lifeless ridges and alkali
deserts that sprawled in the approaches to the
long slopes and frowning escarpments of the
Trinity Mountains.

Unable to shake off the feeling of being jaded
and enervated, Sam soon began to curse the
need for what he was doing. His conscious
mind was no longer convinced of the need for
it—since his stolen gold was his only real
concern and Anstey and Kaufmann were clearly not going to take him anywhere near it this
afternoon—but the subtle impulsion of his
deeper mind remained and, though he would
have liked to turn back and make his peace
with cousin Lucinda, he kept concentrating on
the ride and asking himself what on earth his
quarry could be journeying in this direction for,

53

since there was nothing out this way—except a few abandoned mines from the goldrush days, the Ackerman quartz mill, which had died the death within the last two years, the remnant of a logging claim, and a stretch of the trail that linked the towns of Reno and Fallon; so, what with one thing and another, any urgent business which cousin Charlie and Issy Kaufmann might have in these parts could well be of no real interest to him; though he did remind himself that, as with things good, so with things crooked, everything tended to be of everything else a part, and if Anstey and Kaufmann had done evil in one place today, it was not unlikely that they would follow up that evil with more of the same elsewhere. It was a consideration anyhow, and it belonged with the promptings that his deeper mind was using to keep him on the move.

With short breaks here and there—for the terrain became ever more dry and stony—the well-marked trail left by the two men ahead bore Sam steadily onwards for the better part of another hour and, the altitude of his ride increasing as he approached the ridge above what he was aware to be a long descent to the north of this spot, he realized that he was nearing the low ground crossed by the Reno/Fallon trail and felt a slight quickening of interest because of it; and then he heard gunshots come echoing sullenly at him from the near distance and automatically increased pace, topping out to a view of the Reno/Fallon trail—beyond the shallow slope ahead and more than a mile away—and the stagecoach upon it which had just been stopped by a body of horsemen who were obviously in process of robbing it.

Dismounting, Sam backed his horse out of their stand against the sky and, with the animal hidden by the land, went down on his stomach behind the ridge and began watching the hold-up below, reflecting that, in the dime novels of this day, he would by now be riding hell-for-leather down the gradient, trusty sixgun in his grip, and on the brink of an heroic delivery. Fine! These imaginary deeds of derring-do made great reading. The trouble was, in real life they usually got the hero shot, and he was good and sure that, with the present expanse of wide open ground between him and the road agents, such a fate would be his if he attempted anything so rash. Thus, while he did not regard himself as more of a coward than the next guy, he would be quite happy to spy on what was happening for now and perhaps dog the bandits' trail afterwards.

A mile—and maybe another quarter—was no great distance, but it was sufficient for everything at the end of it to be slightly blurred and diminished to the naked eye, and it took at least a minute for Sam to be sure of his count—as the robbers milled about the stagecoach—but he settled on there being eight road agents at work down there. He had a strong suspicion that Charlie Anstey was among them—for he thought he had glimpsed his cousin's lean, round-shouldered figure on a couple of occasions—but he could not be certain about it, any more than he had managed to form a reliable impression of the looks of any other member of the outlaw gang; and he was as far as ever from making a single reliable identification among the eight badmen when, after a burst of shots to encourage the team pulling the stagecoach to gallop out of the area at top speed, the gangsters rode off in a northeasterly direction and were soon lost to sight behind the rock walls that obscured the trail in the direction from which the coach had come.

Sam thrust himself to his feet again. He would follow the outlaws. It had now become his duty so to do. He must try to make sure whether or not cousin Charlie had joined a team of road agents. If Charlie had done so, then the possibilities for family anguish were unlimited, and it was up to him to put a stop to his cousin's career before some irreparable state materialised. It was a terrible thing that cousin Charlie could have committed criminal acts against him, but highway robbery was something else again. If the worst should happen, and Charlie ended up swinging from the gallows, he would feel that he had failed uncle Bert and aunt Kathy, his only surviving relatives from the senior generation and the two people who had helped him through his grief when his own parents had died of cholera and assisted him to grow up into something like a competent human being. The old pair doted on their son Charlie and, though they must know in their own hearts that he was a bad lot, would never admit that he could do anything wrong.

Leading his horse over the ridge, Sam swung into leather and began riding down the slope towards the trail in the low at the fastest pace that he considered safe in the carpet of scree before them. He made it to the Reno/Fallon trail without mishap, however, then dug in his heels for a real gallop. After that he covered a fast two miles on the road northeastwards, but then eased up on his mount, for he could not overlook the fact that he had been travelling at a far greater speed in recent minutes than had the road agents when they had left the place of the stagecoach robbery. Obviously he must avoid all risk of overtaking the gang, and even that of suddenly appearing in its wake and perhaps getting spotted by some crook who happened to glance back at that moment.

It occurred to him about then that he was getting near the spot where the abandoned Ackerman quartz mill was situated, and in the same instant came the thought that the mill would make a first class hideout. The buildings stood on a low plateau, well back from the trail and with a pinewood between them and it, and were sufficiently remote from the larger centres of population hereabouts almost never to be visited casually. Thus an outlaw band could find relative security up there, a good water supply, and the comfort of staff buildings which had not yet had time to deteriorate all that much from the assault of the elements.

Yes, it was a good notion and he felt intuitively that it ought to be checked out; so, when he rounded the corner which formed the western end of the cliff that had been overhanging him from the right for a minute or two past and saw the quartz mill's approach road running upwards into the pine trees that covered the side of the hill which had appeared on the same hand, he eased back on his reins and turned the animal onto the side road at a much slower pace, leaning down over his right knee as he now progressed upwards and seeing in the dust plenty of evidence that many hooves had travelled on and off the slope in the recent past.

Cautious, but not unduly so, Sam encouraged his mount to pick up speed again and climbed at a steady rate, the shadow of the trees falling upon him now; and, vigilant through every moment, he let the slow left-hand curve of road take him up through the pinewood and towards the mill buildings on the summit above. The flies buzzed and nipped, and the smell of resin made the air so dense that it was difficult to breathe, but the presence of vegetation was a boon after the fields of rock and alkali behind him, and it was with real pleasure that he did, on nearing the hilltop, what seemed wisest and made a left turn off the road, entering the trees and riding slowly onwards through their shade until he came to a circular spot among the rough fir trunks where the grass grew green and thick and the new growth on the berry bushes was still young and tender. Here he halted and, dismounting, ground-tied his horse where it could eat the richest of the grass while he was away. Then he faced upwards again and began following a serpentine path through the wood which brought him out on the southern edge of the plateau and opposite the windowless end wall of the mill building itself.

It was only then that Sam remembered that his gunbelt was still in his saddlebag and that, by habit rather than design, he was still walking unarmed. He thought about going back for his Colt, since he could be in real danger up here, but he wanted to get this over with and did not feel that he had time to waste, so he strode quickly across the space before him— which, according to the rutted surface of the yellow clay, had once been the mill's freight yard—and arrived under the southern wall of the building. Then he sidled to his right and, coming to the corner of the structure at that end, peered round it with caution and looked along the mill's front wall. About half-way along it he saw the building's main doorway, and close to that—on his side—the hitching rail at which numerous horses were tethered. The brutes were swinging their tails at the sandflies that buzzed about them, and their hides alternately glistened with patches of sweat or were dulled by the dirt of travel. The mounts had clearly been tied for only a short while, and Sam had no doubt that they were the animals which had carried their owners to and from the stagecoach robbery that he had witnessed not so long ago.

Sliding round the corner, Sam began advancing along the mill's front wall. He ducked low beneath the several windows on the route and soon came to the main doorway. This he crossed in a flitting movement and, hearing a mutter of male voices which originated from a room directly ahead, stopped under the window there and listened intently, the mutter breaking down into words that had meaning.

Retreating a little, Sam raised his head until he could turn his left eye through the near lower corner of the window beside him and found himself peering into a room that must once have been an office, for there was a big desk against the back wall of the place and there were cupboards and cabinets around of the kind in which clerks kept papers and ledgers and such like. Scattered about the room—and Sam counted them at a single pass of his eye— were eight men, and among them, large as life and twice as ugly, was cousin Charlie, his thin shoulders hunched forward as he sat on a clerk's high-stool and his sharp and shiny nose held at an angle which resembled that of a bird pecking worms. Beside Charlie—darkly fawning as he looked towards the desk—stood a thick-set pudding-faced man who was in need of a shave, and whose round-eyed Semetic look singled him out in the greatest probability as Issy Kaufmann. At the desk—and really the centre of attention for all within the office sat a tall man of exceptional physique and good looks, though his lips were thin in profile and his expression one of natural viciousness. Golden-haired, he sat with his Stetson tipped onto the back of his head and his long-fingered hands riffling through a wad of paper money that had obviously been taken from the blasted strong-box standing on the desk before him. This man was the undoubted boss of the party—just as the money was undoubted loot from the heist down the road—and Sam recognised him from a card table encounter of a year or two ago in Carson City. The fellow was Bray Bebbinger, a much wanted bandit both here in Nevada and over the mountains in California. Thus it was proved. Cousin Charlie was riding with Bray Bebbinger, one-time scourge of the goldfields, master gunman, and a current prince among highwaymen. It was bad. Charlie was well down the road to hell; and this was going to break the hearts of uncle Bert and aunt Kathy—if they found out.

Sam drew away from the window and straightened up. His mission was complete, and there was no sense hanging about. What mattered now was to get safely away from this place and back to Hazewater. He backed across the doorway; then, facing round, he passed down the front of the mill at a light-footed run, turning right when he reached the corner at its southern end and then slanting with no loss of pace towards the point at the edge of the plateau from which he had come up from the pinewood on that side when first approaching the structure now at his back. After that, entering the trees agin, he moved downwards at a checked run in the direction of the circle of grass in which he had left his horse, and had the animal in sight through the boles, when a bearded man of enormous size stepped into his path from behind an evergreen bush, his thick lips and piggy eyes grinning with wicked delight as he pointed his Winchester and rasped: 'Not so fast, my beauty! You hold it right there!'

Jerking to a halt, Sam held it—right there.

CHAPTER FOUR

But Sam stood rooted for a second only. Sensing that the big man was too sure of himself and moving too slowly because of it, he lashed out with his right foot, the toe of his boot aimed at the front underside of the rifle's stock, and so good was his aim and his kick so powerful that the weapon was torn from his challenger's grasp and went sailing into the trees on the giant's right.

Startled by the speed and manner of his dispossession, the big fellow—one of Bray Bebbinger's gangsters, Sam presumed, probably left throughout the afternoon to watch over the site of the quartz mill as its roving guard—glanced involuntarily in the direction in which his Winchester had gone, and Sam seized his chance, walking into the other with both fists swinging.

He landed a tremendous left hook to the jaw, and then a heavy right cross, repeating the blows time after time as the giant staggered backwards, with arms outflung; then, gathering himself and measuring his punches with a care that he could now afford, he struck alternately for the point of the chin, and the bearded man was in the act of falling before the barrage, when his upper back caught against the trunk of a tree and received the kind of bracing that was needed to keep him upright. Dazed, he stood thus, with his knees shaking and blood running into his beard; and, frustrated and swearing, Sam jumped in close and tried to complete the big fellow's collapse with a short left to the midriff and a heavy shove from the right.

Gasping, the giant heeled over onto his right knee, but prevented himself from spreading his length by thrusting out his right hand and creating a new support. Sam eased off for a moment to draw breath and gather himself for a really destroying blow; but this time the other saw his chance and, after fumbling behind his left hip, came lurching erect with a well—honed Bowie knife advanced at his opponent's stomach.

Sam realized at once that he was too near the knife. He bounded to the rear as the big man slashed at him. The tip of the knife raked the buckle of his belt but did no harm. Then the other started to chop and slash obliquely, advancing now, and Sam sprang this way and that to avoid the cutting edge—but knew that sooner or later he would feel the steel bite if he allowed the big guy to persist. Yet for all his show of energy, the giant was obviously far from clear-headed, and his efforts began to grow wild as the smaller man's evasive movements continued to thwart him. Then he lunged, trying to stab, and his toe came into contact with a surfaced pine-root, the jar of it throwing him badly off balance; and, as he stumbled forward, bent at the waist and with the point of his knife slanted back at himself, Sam stepped in with both hands clenched and lifted well above the level of his crown. Then he slammed his fists down on the giant's nape with all his weight and strength, and the other fell heavily onto his face, giving vent to a low, gurgling cry, and then he tipped convulsively onto his back, revealing that the Bowie knife had buried itself eight inches deep in his diaphragm and that he was dying. A final shudder passed through the man from head to heel, and then Sam stood gasping above an empty human shell which sprawled limply and now began bleeding over the grass.

Feeling sick at the stomach, Sam staggered to his horse and freed it; then, after looking round to make sure that they were once more alone in the trees, he mounted up. Now he threw the corpse a final glance. He hadn't really wanted to kill the big varmint, but it had happened, and you could not bring a dead man back to life. Best take advantage of what he had gained. 'Come on, horse,' he ordered, and they moved off through the trees, following the hillside downwards for a couple of hundred yards before bearing left and emerging on the quartz mill's approach road at a point that was hidden from the plateau above by the bend in the way. They soon cleared the pinewood after that, and the rest of the descent made no demands on them at all.

Back on the Reno/Fallon trail, they clattered southwestwards at a place that ought to put them beyond all risk of being overtaken by pursuers—even should the giant's body be more or less immediately found by Bebbinger's gang—within a matter of ten or fifteen minutes; and by the time Sam reached the place where the stagecoach had been robbed earlier that afternoon, with an empty road at his back, he felt reasonably sure that he was now safe from all the consequences of his spying mission at the Ackerman quartz mill.

But it never paid to take chances that you didn't have to take, as he was always telling himself, so he kept his horse moving at a faster pace than he liked as he began his traverse of the arid scene beyond the trail and made for Hazewater, his thoughts once more reverting to the subject of cousin Charlie and what to do about him.

That he must give the hellion a chance was plain as a pikestaff. But what form was that chance to take. Charlie was the kind of cranky, light-minded individual who could not be trusted to stick to any agreement once it had outrun its immediate value to him. He could well do his level best for his cousin—even to the extent of putting himself in danger from the law—and then get severely let down. Thinking back, Sam could remember a number of occasions when Charlie had betrayed friends and helpers, behaving as if he had neither conscience nor honour and was the only man who mattered. A guy like that did not change and, being fair about it, giving him chances was really an offence against other people. Had it been a straightforward business—without uncle Bert and aunt Kathy having to be considered—he would have seen Charlie in jail before the day was out, and not given a cuss what happened to him beyond that point. But he could not let the old pair think that he did not care about them, and protecting their ne'er-do-well son was one way of showing that he did. His mind was made up; but there was no clever way of doing it. He would simply ride to the Anstey home now, and ask for the opportunity to speak with Charlie when he arrived back at the cottage.

Not that Sam meant, in favouring his cousin, to let the rest of the Bebbinger gang escape justice. By no means! He would call on the sheriff and tell almost all of what he had seen, but it did look as if that call would have to be delayed until the morning; for he now perceived that, with captured outlaws being the greatest betrayers of their own kind, he must give Charlie time to ride out of the district before having the Bebbinger gang brought in.

Sam was aware that his horse was tuckered out as they completed the last leg of their return to the Anstey cottage a little over an hour later. Dismounting, he tied his horse at his uncle's hitching rail, then went in through the gate again and walked up to the dwelling beyond. Here he rat-tatted on the front door, then folded his arms and stood waiting for somebody to answer. He heard footfalls coming towards him through the house only a few moments later. Then the door opened and cousin Lucinda peered out at him, surprise leaping into her eyes; but this expression turned almost instantly into one of angry contempt and she said: 'Oh, it's you, is it? I suppose you've come crawling back to beg my pardon?'

'I've come back,' Sam said evenly. 'No crawling, and your pardon I will not beg, since I see no cause. Have your ma and papa got home yet?'

'No, they're still out visitin',' Lucinda answered, 'and likely to be till dark.'

'Can I come in?'

'All offers are off, Sam.'

'They were never on so far as I was concerned.'

'Changed man, are we?' she jeered.

'See it as you like,' he said flatly. 'Can I come in, Lucinda?'

'What for?'

'To wait for your brother. I must talk to Charlie when he gets home.'

'To?' she asked acutely. 'Not with?'

'To,' he said, playing her at her own tight game. 'And must.'

'*Must?*'

'Exactly.'

'You didn't catch up with him and Issy Kaufmann while you were out?' Lucinda questioned uncertainly.

'No—though I did glimpse him one time.'

'If you were able to do that much, why couldn't you speak to him?'

'Look, Lucinda,' Sam said patiently. 'Your

brother is in bad trouble. For the sake of your ma and pa, I want to save him from the consequences of it. Yes, and your sake too.'

'Trouble?' Lucinda echoed, paling as she stepped aside. 'Come on in, then. You hadn't better start trying to take advantage, Sam. I'll have the sheriff after you.'

'Moses!' Sam breathed, walking into the passage behind the front door and then turning into the parlour through the entrance that was situated on his almost immediate left.

The girl entered the low-ceilinged little room in his wake. Then, moving around him as he stopped before the table at the middle of the floor, she went to the hearth and there turned to face him again, pointing at the sofa and inviting him to sit down.

Sam was glad to accept the invitation and sank tiredly onto the seat. 'Have you got a glass of water?' he asked, running his tongue around a mouth which felt like the interior of an old boot.

'We've got some lager beer.'

He gave his head a shake. 'Water will do fine.'

'Tell me about the trouble that Charlie's in,' she said, as she left the room and headed for the kitchen, which was just a few paces along

71

the passage. 'I can hear you well enough through here.'

'I'd rather not lift my voice all the same,' Sam said, hearing her dip a glass into the bucket of drinking water which he knew to stand just inside the pantry.

Lucinda reappeared with a glass of rather cloudy-looking water in her grasp. 'If you must be so all-fired careful,' she remarked, 'I suppose you must.'

'That's how it is,' he acknowledged, accepting the glass from her hand and drinking until it was empty.

'Thanks.'

She took the glass from him and stood it on the mantelpiece.

Sam saw no point in mincing his words, and plunged straight in. 'The fool's riding with Bray Bebbinger's gang.' He went on to tell her about the stagecoach robbery which he had witnessed during the afternoon and of the things that he had more recently seen at the old Ackerman quartz mill, ending: 'I can't hide what I know, Lucinda. That would be a crime. I must carry my information to Sheriff Jack Stockman, and the best I can do is delay my call on him until the morning. That should give Charlie time to get away.'

The girl had lowered her gaze to the floor,

and she was biting her bottom lip. It seemed to the watching Sam that she was neither as shocked nor surprised as she ought to have been by his words. But then she reacted in a manner that was far more sudden and startling than he could have expected. 'Why couldn't you keep your nose out?' she flared, her eyes jerking level and seeming to rake him with the fires generated in their somewhat murky depths. 'Sam, you've always been a spyin', self-righteous varmint, and now—and now you've been an' gone and done this to poor Charlie!'

'Poor Charlie's done it to himself,' Sam reminded her. 'It's a bit harsh to go for me when I'm doing my best for all of you. I'm not self-righteous. As for the g'damn spyin'—! Well, it's forced on a man sometimes.'

'You've always been like it!' she accused. 'You're a shame to the family! Everybody in Hazewater knows what you are! You're a lazy good-for-nothing! All you think about, when you're not traipsin' around the country with a pick and shovel, is getting into bed with any girl who'll risk it and drinking rot-gut whisky in Henry Bellarion's place! You're a disgrace, Sam Cade—an absolute disgrace to us all!' Then she dissolved into noisy blubbering, and went round the room stamping her left foot at intervals and shaking her fists in the air.

Sam allowed the worst of the storm to pass, then let out a sigh and said: 'I guess you're upset, Lucinda, and have got to take it out on somebody. I'm duly elected.'

'You're no good!'

'As for what you say about me,' he said heavily, 'it's only a tinge true, and you know it. I've had my fun, but I've paid well for it—and I've harmed nobody. I didn't know everybody cared so much about what I'm supposed to be and, what's more, I don't believe they do.' He paused, then reached out and gave her a playful pat on the rump which contained elements of sympathy and conciliation. 'Anyhow, girl, whatever's wrong in my life doesn't put right what's wrong in Charlie's; and he's still up to his neck in trouble.'

'I guess so,' Lucinda gulped, her attitude becoming noticeably less hostile as she knuckled at her wet eyes. 'Ma and pa mustn't hear anything of this.'

'Now we're speaking the same language,' Sam agreed, though he could perceive circumstances looming in which it might not be possible to avoid uncle Bert and aunt Kathy hearing what their son had been up to if he were forced to repeat his revelations after they had returned home. 'If we're lucky, Charlie will get back first and we'll be able to do our talking while your ma and papa are still out.'

Lucinda was very quiet for a moment; and then she said: 'It occurs to me, Sam, that I ought to handle this. Let me talk to Charlie. I'll give a full account of what you've said, and let him know he's warned. You can go about your business.'

'No,' Sam said. 'Reckon not.'

'You haven't thought of everything,' the girl pointed out. 'Issy Kaufmann will be with my brother. Issy has to bring my horse back.'

'There is that,' Sam admitted, wondering how he had missed it for so long. 'Could alter it some.'

'Would alter it lots. They're inseparable here. Do you want Issy to have the same chance as Charlie?'

'No,' Sam answered. 'I ain't that dead set on harming Kaufmann, Lucinda, but I've got him pegged for a wicked influence that your brother would be better without. I've also got to consider what the guy could carry to Bray Bebbinger. That's a thorny one.'

'If you're here,' Lucinda persisted, 'Charlie will insist whatever you say to him is heard by Issy as well.'

'Could happen like that, I suppose.'

'Then you must leave it to me.'

Sam put a hand to his brow. There was his gold; he must keep that squarely in mind. He must not abandon his own interests entirely out of concern for the Ansteys. His gold had not come that easily, and it meant a great deal to him. 'Oh, hell!' he exploded, confessing to himself the full extent of his exasperation. 'If only it could be as easy as you make it sound. There's more to it, Lucinda, and what there is concerns me personally. Because of that, I ought to talk to Charlie face to face.'

'Why didn't you speak about this before?' the girl asked sharply. 'Tell me about it. I can put whatever it is to Charlie, can't I? If there's some answer you must have, I'll bring it to you wherever you're staying.'

'Won't really do,' Sam said. 'It's not that I don't trust you, mind. It's just that I can't trust how it might work out if it was done like that. No, if I let you handle it—'

'You *don't* trust me,' she interrupted bitterly.

He hated the none too subtle pressure that she was putting on him. It wouldn't do, but it would have to do, for he needed her as an ally and, if he didn't let her do what she wished-ed, he would only make a complete enemy of her. 'All right, then. But you must tell Charlie to come and see me before he leaves town.'

'Where will you be staying, Sam?'

76

'Ma Beamish's place. My usual room.'

'I'll tell Charlie to come there.'

'Make sure he does,' Sam warned, rising to his feet. 'There's a lot riding on it. And I promise you this. If he slides off without coming to see me, I'll hound him from one side of this country to the other before I let him get away with it.'

'Get away with—what?' Lucinda queried.

'Doesn't matter. You've got your victory. Just tell him what I said.'

She pouted. 'You make it sound so serious.'

'It's good and serious,' Sam assured her. 'Now you be careful, Lucinda. I've an idea you already know a lot more about Charlie's affairs than you're letting on. That could be real dangerous, how things are.'

The girl looked furtive. 'I'll see you to the door.'

'No need,' he said, leaving the parlour, opening the front door, and pausing to add over his shoulder: 'I think we understand each other. I'll be in to see uncle Bert and aunt Kathy some time. So long.'

' 'Bye, Sam,' she answered from the parlour.

Sam shut the door behind him. Then he began walking towards the front gate and the lane beyond it; but he was still several paces short of the exit, when cousin Charlie came

77

shoving onto the property, eyes down and looking every inch the villain that he was. He glanced up quickly, however, on sensing Sam's presence and, as their eyes met, his jaws fell open, his cheeks turned ashen, and he began to shake. 'You!' he breathed. 'It can't be you! You're dead!'

'Bo-hoooo!' Sam moaned, raising his hands above his head and fluttering his fingers. 'I am the ghost of Samuel Cade, and I've come to haunt you!'

Cousin Charlie went for his gun. Sam stepped in promptly and hit his cousin flush on the jaw with an enormous right that started from behind his ear. Knocked completely senseless, Charlie fell onto his back and lay stiff as board.

'Bo-hoooo!' Sam moaned. 'You—bastard!'

CHAPTER FIVE

Standing over the unconscious man, Sam looked towards the gate in the expectation that Issy
Kaufmann was about to come through it, but
the man didn't appear and Cade's senses told
him that there was nobody else in the vicinity.
Satisfied that he could act safely, Sam grabbed
his cousin by the heels and dragged Charlie in
the direction of the cottage—where a glance
back showed him that Lucinda must have seen
what had happened through the parlour window and was now blubbering at the open front
door—and, reaching the girl, he elbowed her
aside and then hauled her senseless brother into
the dwelling and through to the kitchen, where
he released Charlie's feet and let him lie, then
turned to the pantry and brought out the
bucket of drinking water, emptying the three
or four gallons that it contained straight over
Charlie's head and shoulders.

Charlie came spluttering back to his senses.
He sat up, cursing and swearing, and wiped
at his soaked upper body with hands that were

soon equally wet. 'Lay off!' he howled, as he saw Sam standing there. But there was no respite, for Sam seized him by the front of his shirt and heaved him to his feet. Then, with cries of 'Get up thar', he booted his cousin all the way round the kitchen, out into the passage, and then through to the parlour, where he gave him a last and especially hard kick which sent him nosediving into the fireplace. Here he ended up with his head thrust into the bottom of the chimney and soot pouring down on him from above.

'Oh, Cousin Sam!' the onlooking Lucinda wailed from the doorway of the room. 'Oh, Cousin Sam!'

'Yeah,' Sam agreed sourly. 'I'm a cruel fellow, Lucinda; but, if I'd given that brother of yours what's really due to him, he'd be work for the sexton now and food for the worms.'

. 'Hellion!' Charlie Anstey raged, withdrawing from the chimney and heaving over to sit on the hearth, his red tongue sticking out of features so caked with soot that he looked like a nigger minstrel. 'You hellion, Sam Cade!'

The man made another move for his gun. Sam dived foward. He snatched the weapon out of his cousin's grasp. Then he open the Colt's loading gate and spun out the contents of its cylinder over the floor, casting the emptied weapon on the couch after that. 'What d' you say now?' he asked disdainfully. 'Will you never learn?'

Charlie rose to his feet, a sight to behold as he held his bruised posterior and cursed and swore like a man possessed.

'You foul-mouthed coyote!' Sam exclaimed. 'I really can't think why I should have gone to such lengths on your behalf. I've just been talking to your sister about it. I know you're riding with Bray Bebbinger, and I know you took part in a stage robbery this afternoon. I could have gone straight to the sheriff, Charlie. Should have gone. But I've come here instead to give you a chance.' He screwed up his mouth, only resisting the impulse to spit as he realized that this was his uncle's house. 'I love and respect your ma and papa, boy, but you're a rogue through and through.'

'Good on yuh, Sammy!' Charlie sneered. 'Now what's the catch?'

'I want my gold,' Sam answered flatly. 'I want those sacks of ore that you and Kaufmann robbed me of this morning. Once I've got those, you can go wherever the wind takes a foul smell like you.' He cast a glance over his shoulder. 'By the way, where is that fellow Issy Kaufmann?'

'He's gone to fetch his horse from the black-

81

smith's shop,' Charlie replied. 'He left yours at the gate, sis.'

'It was that loose hoof-iron that put me on to you,' Sam informed him. 'I picked it up at the spot outside town where Kaufmann's nag threw it. Then I had a little talk with Gerry Stubbs. That talk led me here, and after that I followed the tracks you and Issy left out to the Reno/Fallon trail—and later to the Ackerman quartz mill. I saw Bebbinger counting out the loot there, with you flea-bittin lot looking on.'

'Clever, ain't you?' Charlie snarled.

'Not even slightly,' Sam retorted. 'All I want's for you to know how well I know what I know.'

Sniffing, Charlie wiped his nose on his sleeve.

'What's this talk about gold, Charlie?' Lucinda demanded.

'In a hurry, ain't we?' Charlie jeered. 'Maybe there ain't no gold. Supposin' I say he's got it all wrong?'

'Charlie,' Sam said, in his quietest and most deadly voice, 'if you take that line—or start getting obstructive—I'm going to beat the living daylight out of you. You know me for a man of my word. I'm the mildest of men in most circumstances—in fact too easy-going for my own good—but I can be an old-fashioned berserker when my temper's up, and I'm awful strong. So you heed me when I say that if I start in on you, you may never walk again—or see again—or even want to reach next week. Don't you—don't you even think of not telling me where my gold is.'

'Sam, you're plain awful!' Lucinda announced, howling yet again.

'Seems we're a right wicked family,' Sam agreed implacably. 'Well, Charlie?'

'Ain't no need for you to be getting worked up like that, Sam,' Charlie said, grinning a frightened, sickly grin through the soot which disfigured his face. 'I'm not denyin' anything. Who says I'm worried? Getting a fire-assay is job enough, but the sellin' of the ore afterwards can be mighty ticklish. I never did go all the way with Issy's plan to rob you from the start. But he would have it, and he fired that rifle before I could stop him.' He paused, trying to look contrite, but merely adding to his general air of shiftiness. 'You can have your gold, Sam, and I'll be pleased to see you get it, but you'll never drop on where them mules are hidden just by my telling it. I'll have to take you there. After dark. Issy would skin me if he saw what I was about. Soon as I've shown you where your gold is, Sam, I'll ride for the mountains. There's a heap more room in California.'

'Now you're being smart, Charlie!' Sam applauded. 'You may depend upon it that I shan't mention your name when I tell Sheriff Stockman what I know about Bray Bebbinger and his gang. Was I you, I'd stay out of Nevada for a year or two. Folk have mercifully short memories, and the law's not inclined to do much if the evidence is lacking. I see no reason why yours should be a permanent exile. However, that'll be up to you.'

'Decision for when the time comes,' Charlie said. 'Ma and pa won't like it, but I've talked before today about going away to seek m' fortune. They'll just have to look sad.'

'Better than weeping,' Sam reminded meaningfully. 'Where do we meet, Charlie, and at what time?'

'There's a big sycamore on the western edge of town,' Charlie responded. 'You know the one. Some say it was used as a hangin' tree back a bit.'

'I know it.'

'Be under it, with your hoss, around half ten,' Charlie instructed. 'Should be no problem to leave town unseen at that hour. On the other hand, it's comin' up to the full moon, so we should have plenty of light for riding in the country.'

'I'll be there,' Sam assured him. 'See that

you are. Now get yourself a wash. You look like a tar baby.'

'Family difference,' Charlie smirked.

'Have you done, Sam?' Lucinda asked.

Sam gave his head a jerk. 'For now.'

'Thought you had,' the girl said, looking pointedly at the door.

Nodding again, and leaving the brother and sister standing there, Sam walked out of the room; and, as he left the house, he was conscious that they hated him badly enough for anything; but he couldn't help that, for when trying to do the right made enemies, those enemies had to stand.

Passing into the lane outside the cottage, Sam untied his horse from the Anstey hitching rail and then walked the brute back into the Hazewater main street, where he let it drink its fill at the trough outside the barber's shop. Then he walked the animal a short distance eastwards and halted outside Ma Beamish's rooming house. Here he tied the horse at a picket fence on the right of the property, and then went up to Freda Beamish's front door, his knock producing the good lady herself and a few words the understanding that he was to be a paying guest in her house on a day-to-day basis. In confirmation of their agreement Sam paid one dollar in advance.

Sam had, of course, stayed in Ma Beamish's house many times before, and it took him just five minutes to settle in. After that he went out and got himself a meal, and then he returned to his room, kicked off his boots, had a yawn and scratch, stretched himself out on the bed, and went to sleep; and thus he remained until the grandfather clock down in the hall clanked off the hour of ten, when he got up, shook himself together, had a wash, pulled his boots back on, and then went clumping downstairs again and out to the picket fence, where he found his horse waiting for him much as he had left it.

After leading the animal onto the street, Sam swung into the saddle and set off slowly westwards, his gaze moving back and forth more in interest than anticipation. On his left hung the moon, an almost perfect disc of oily yellow, and the town lay spectral in the layer of gloom under its light. Ahead of him, way beyond the spot where the rooftops seemed to converge, scarlet threads of the afterglow still lingered amidst the Californian thunderheads, and he rode towards this dim field of splintered radiance with a sense of dreaming, but presently the black swell of the land's nearer contours cut out the view and he reached the western limit of the town and rode those extra yards which brought him to the sycamore tree that Charlie had given as their meeting place.

Sam halted under the tree. Remaining in his saddle, he lifted his hands to a bough that was within reach and took a grip on it, stretching himself pleasantly between timber and stirrups. He judged that the time must be nearing ten-thirty p.m., and wondered whether Charlie would be punctual—if, indeed, he appeared at all, for Sam was far from easy about what he was doing tonight. Charlie was as crafty as a waggon load of monkeys, as ruthless as the next man with no moral sense, and undoubtedly smarting from his general failure and the hiding that he had received from his cousin. This didn't have to go well, and Sam wasn't so blind that he didn't know it. There were options, and they lay with Charlie. If the man's cowardice broke down for once, he could try to spring something half-smart, and Sam realized that he must remain in a state of high vigilance until the night was over. Even when he had parted from Charlie—assuming everything went according to plan—and he had the gold back in his possession, he must not take it for granted that he was safe.

It was probably a few minutes after the time arranged when Sam heard the sounds of a horse approaching at his back and craned to see a rider coming up through the hazy moonlight. 'That you, Charlie?' he inquired in a normal tone of voice.

'It's me,' came the reply. 'Been waiting long?'

Now that was a considerate question, and Charlie sounded quite anxious about it. 'I haven't been here long,' Sam replied. 'How did your ma and pa take it?'

'How the hell d'you think they took it?'

Sam smiled to himself. That was more like Charlie. It wasn't good for bad 'un's to begin talking out of character too soon. This business of turning over new leaves—supposing Charlie was capable of it—should not come too quickly. Charlie's mount trotted by him now, and Sam gigged forward, reaching enough speed within the moment to catch up with the other and then ease back at his right elbow. 'Could be the making of you, boy. It's all up to you.'

'Blast you, Sam! You're so good and right-eous!'

'You know I'm not.'

'Then lay off playin' Holy Joe,' Charlie cautioned. 'I ain't in the mood for any more lectures. Pa figured something was up—because Lucinda and me was so close-mouthed—and he led off real strong. So did ma, when she wasn't sheddin' tears. And it's all your fault, damn

88

you! You won't be getting any more of the goodies from Lucinda, I can tell you that—'cos she plumb hates you!'

'Tell me somethin' new,' Sam pleaded. 'My fault, eh? Charlie, that ain't new either. That's how these things get twisted round.'

'All you had to do was keep your nose out of my business.'

'You'll get that stuffed right down your gullet if you ain't careful!' Sam warned angrily. 'Have you forgotten what you and Issy Kaufmann did to me this morning? It's known as attempted murder! And that was only half of it. Do attempted murder and robbery suddenly seem like small change to you?' He swallowed his spittle, still seething. 'I had the right to follow you, man! Try putting the blame where it belongs—on yourself. You're a would-be killer and highwayman, and you already deserve to be hanged. Let's not hear another word about the injuries you figure you've been done by a guy you've wronged as badly as me!'

'You're breaking my heart!' Charlie gurgled evilly. 'How the hell did you survive anyhow? I'd have sworn that bullet had gone clean through your heart, and it's a fall of three or four hundred feet to the bottom of Ute Canyon.'

'Charlie,' Sam said, 'I feel worse about you

every minute. You put the blame on Issy Kaufmann for my attempted murder. But something tells me now it was you who did the
shooting. And it just figures—don't it?—that
you knowing so much about me and *my* affairs
has to mark you for the guy who thought up
the crime. As to how I survived—God's mercy
saved me, Charlie boy! May sometimes be
known as Aztec magic, but I'm not going to
shout off my mouth about that. Fact is, I'm
still alive and staying—and you're still alive and
goin'. But there's a heap of gold ore between
us, and that's what matters to me. When it's
back where it belongs, you can burn for all I
care. Got it?'

'You button your lip, Sam!' Charlie snarled.
'I'm better with a sixgun than you are, and if
you go on like this—!'

'Don't get too brave, sonny!' Sam cut in. 'A
fast draw ain't everything. I could shoot the
heart out of you—'cos I've got the guts to stand
there and do it—and I will if you threaten
guns.'

'Shut up!'

'Be glad to,' Sam responded. 'Talking to you
is the worst chore yet. How far?'

'Four miles.'

'Even more glad.'

After that they climbed into the high places

to the south of Hazewater with the silence seeming to fester about them, and Sam was now certain that his cousin would never be numbered among the penitents— much less those who could take their medicine without kicking—and he watched Charlie ever more intently as the miles went by, for, in view of this enlightenment, he was also sure that his cousin would yet make a second attempt to do him mortal damage.

Time went by, and Sam supposed they must have covered about the four miles of which Charlie had spoken, when Anstey made a right turn across his path and said: 'That way.'

Sam touched right rein. They rode off the trail which they had been pursuing across the heights near Ute Canyon and struck off down a fairly shallow slope that appeared to sprawl northwards for miles. The moon's sinister shadows thickened about them as they progressed, but they had in fact dropped little more than a hundred feet below their previous level of travel, when they came to a large clump of growth that had the look and odour of man-zanita about it. Here they turned right across the base of the clump; then, pulling tightly on the same hand, pierced the vegetation to a depth of some yards before moving out into the back of the deep bay that it concealed within the face of the slope.

A small quantity of moonlight filtered to them through the foliage. In this dim gleam, Sam made out a low cliff at the rear of the bay. He saw Charlie swing down near the rockface. Dismounting himself, he lifted his nose and sniffed. Water. A good supply of it, he'd say. When a man spent most of his days in the dry and dusty corners of the earth to which mining led him, he got to recognise that wonderful smell and to appreciate how all life depended on water. 'This another hideout?' he asked.

'Sort of, sort of,' Charlie replied; and then he walked up to the rockface and seemed to disappear through it. 'Come on.'

Sam followed the other. Now his night-conditioned eyes picked out a spot where the stone before him seemed to have depth but reflected nothing. He thought there must be an opening at that point and, thrusting his head forward, found that he was right, since he moved into space and heard the bubbling echoes of spring waters falling back at him from the walls of the cave which now enclosed him.

Sniffing again, Sam detected a second odour, and this was one far more pungent than that of water. Mules—stinking creatures! Well, whatever doubts he had had before, Charlie seemed to have dealt with him honestly this far, for the mules that he could smell were most probably his own; and where they were, his gold would almost certainly be found.

Then a match flared, and Charlie again stood in sight, the sulphur tip's tiny flame leaping and dancing in his upraised right hand. Sam looked around him in the faint glow and saw the irregular walls of a cavern that was perhaps twelve feet deep by ten across, and possibly eight feet high. The spring was situated on his left, and the waters rose out of several tiny vents at the bottom of a sandstone basin and flowed away into a natural drain near the front of the cave. The mules were standing on his right, and all three were chewing contentedly at the remains of a heap of fodder that appeared to have been hastily spread for them, almost certainly at the time they had been brought here and placed in hiding.

Charlie stepped right up to the back wall of the cave. Sam watched him reach out with his free hand and pick up an almost new candle which lay on a rock shelf at the level of his chest. Touching off the candle's wick from his match, Charlie shook the latter out and let it fall to the floor, encouraging the former to burn its brightest, then stood the candle in a bed of grease that had collected at the front of the shelf and turned to Sam, jerking his chin in the direction of the mules. 'There's your consarned gold,' he said. 'The mules are just as you loaded them.'

'I can see it,' Sam acknowledged. 'I know my own knots.'

'Satisfied!'

'Yes. Go when you like.'

'Just like that, eh?'

'Am I expected to thank you?'

'You're a hard man, Sam.'

'And you know best what you are.'

Charlie let out a contemptuous laugh. 'You damned fool, Sam!' he exclaimed. 'I've let you act big and push me around, but you don't even rate in my game.'

Just then Sam sensed movement at the entrance to the cave, and an instant later he heard a stone roll away from the toe that kicked it. Twisting his head towards the opening, he glimpsed a man's figure bowed there, and then made out the Semitic features of the man who could only be Issy Kaufmann above the barrel of the revolver that pointed at him.

CHAPTER SIX

Reckoning that he had about half a second to live, Sam jumped. He jumped right behind cousin Charlie's back and pulled the other to him with his left arm. Then he plucked Charlie's pistol out of its holster and fired three rapid shots towards the muzzle of the gun opposite, which was already vomiting redly in an effort to kill him. He felt Charlie stiffen, then begin to sag and, releasing his hold on the villain, let him crumple to the floor. After that Sam dived for the exit, bent on pursuing the now vanished Kaufmann, whom he was pretty sure he had hit at least with his first shot.

Once out of the cave, Sam heard his enemy in full retreat several yards beyond him and, shoving by a horse—Charlie's or his own—that came skittering into his path and neighing its fright, he forced his way through the vegetation that covered the bay and emerged on the slope beyond, staggering to a halt and at a loss for the direction that Kaufmann had taken.

He threw glances about him. The merging

details of the moonscape baffled his eyes. Then a gun flashed at him from somewhere to his right and high. A bullet whispered above his head. Glancing over the point of his right shoulder, he perceived Kaufmann's shape standing about thirty yards away. Turning to face the man, Sam extended his right arm and aimed a trifle high, squeezing off a shot that he felt was a good one, and the next moment he saw the badman go reeling backwards and heard him give vent to a small, gasping scream. He had Issy pegged for a dead man, and expected the other to fall, but Kaufmann surprised him by recovering and facing about, after which he laboured up the slope that reached to the south of him and appeared to be heading for a cluster of boulders that stood not more than twenty yards beyond the spot at which he had received the bullet.

Again exercising care with his aim, Sam tried another shot, but heard his lead wail off stone and knew that he had fired a miss. He triggered once more, but his hammer fell on a fired chamber and he realized that the weapon in his hand needed reloading. Standing his ground now, Sam was unsure as to what was going to happen next. He felt the urge to go pelting after Kaufmann, but he also felt the need to return to the cave and find out whether cousin Charlie was still alive. He no longer feared Kaufmann in any sense of the word, for instinct told him that the badman was severely hurt and incapable of further fighting, but he did recognise the slight danger that he could be wrong and wanted to be sure that the other was completely out of the reckoning before he let his battle concentration slip. Then the situation crystalised, for Sam heard a horse scrambling into motion, and a moment later he saw Kaufmann heave into view, and go riding over the upper part of the slope and head for the trail on the ridge above. The villain reached the top of his climb within half a minute, drew left and then headed eastwards, only the mutter of his flight remaining shortly after that.

Now Sam ran back into the manzanita and re-entered the cave which it concealed. The candle was still burning at the rear of the rock chamber, and he could see exactly where his cousin lay. He threw Charlie's pistol aside; then, going to the prostrate man, he knelt beside him and turned him onto his back. Charlie looked dead, but wasn't quite, for his eyes blinked open and, despite their strangely vacant stare, he recognised Sam and muttered aggrievedly: 'You used me as a shield.'

'That I did,' Sam admitted. 'Fair's fair, Charlie. You set me up. That was poor. I wasn't even wearing a gun. It was you and yours—or nothing.'

'Issy?'

'He's hit—but away.'

'That was his—'

'No Charlie,' Sam cautioned. 'A lie will surely bear you to hell.'

'You're right,' Charlie confessed. 'It was my idea. From the first, what's been done to you was all my idea. I told Issy to ride out here and await our—our coming. I figured if we did it like that you wouldn't get any—any feeling of being followed.'

'I could see that you had options,' Sam said, 'but I could only trust.'

Charlie suffered a spasm. 'I'm gut-shot.'

Sam grimaced. 'It won't hurt for long.'

Charlie stared up at him for a few moments longer; and then it was obvious that his agony was indeed over; for the light went out in his gaze and his throat rattled.

'So long, Charlie,' Sam said, closing the dead man's eyes and straightening his limbs. 'I guess I ought to say that I forgive you, but I can't. You were rotten as they come, and you got what you deserved. That's that.'

Rising again, Sam inspected the still eating mules, then stood near the entrance to the cave and gave some thought as to whether or not he should take the corpse and his gold into Hazewater now; but there was the practical problem of what he was to do with the ore once he got it to town at this hour of the night, and Charlie's death would also present another set of complications that would be easier to deal with in daylight. Thus, only too aware that his prime duty was now to call in at the sheriff's office and report where Bray Bebbinger and company could be found, he decided to leave the gold where it was and the body too. He could as easily pick up both tomorrow as now and, by then, events would have digested in his mind and he would be able to answer questions as to what had happened here more clearly. When possible it was always wiser to tackle things by stages. The body and mind preferred it like that, and it also made a better impression on those looking in.

Walking to the rear of the cave, Sam blew out the candle. Then he groped his way slowly out of the place. The two horses were still standing in the bay, and both were motionless again. Reaching towards the pair, he identified his own by tactile impressions, then led it out through the manzanita and onto the slope beyond—leaving Charlie's mount as another item to be collected on the morrow—and after that he stepped into his saddle and headed

99

upwards in the direction of the trail on the ridge, turning eastwards when he reached it and then riding for Hazewater at that sort of medium pace that caused his horse the least fatigue and allowed him the full use of his eyes for observation purposes, since he had the notion that he might come upon Issy Kaufmann's body before long. But this did not happen, and as he neared Hazewater, he knew that it was not going to happen—for Kaufmann had clearly turned across the land somewhere, with or without a set destination in mind—but this was suddenly of minor concern, since it was the totally unexpected that occurred next. For he was still a half mile from town, when a band of horsemen came surging at him out of rocky hiding places along the sides of the trail and forced him to rein back, the moonlight glimmering on their levelled gun barrels. 'I see,' he commented, the muscles of his throat aching with shock and his heart thumping. 'Bray Bebbinger and company.'

'That's us,' agreed the tallest of the dark figures who sat their horses around him. 'You've made enemies of me and my friends, Cade. Seems to me I recall you—from Carson City a while ago—and what I recall doesn't make me happy either. Another score to repay, eh?'

'If you hadn't been a damned cheat at cards,' Sam retorted, 'I wouldn't have had to let on you were dealing "shiners".'

'You saw it,' Bebbinger said, his approval somewhat grudging. 'You could have made good money yourself as a tinhorn.'

'A game's a game,' Sam retorted. 'A living is something you work for.'

'What drivel,' Bebbinger commented. 'You're a man with something in his noodle, Cade, but you've no judgement. Brains without judgment are like a gun without bullets.'

'Maybe I'm too trusting,' Sam sighed. 'But that's not to say I don't recognise possibilities.' Though he knew the chance element had played no part in this, for only one person could have betrayed him to Bebbinger, and that was cousin Lucinda who, for all his effort to placate her, had obviously gone through with her stated intention of getting her own back on him for that little matter of the afternoon. 'I was afraid it'd turn out that Lucinda Anstey didn't only know about her brother's crooked doings but was part of them.'

'What *are* you on about, Cade?' Bebbinger inquired mockingly. 'Irrelevances, mixed tenses, sweet girls out of nowhere. I'm afraid for you, son. Have you been chewing peyote?—or are you full of booze?'

'Neither the one nor the other!' Sam retorted. 'You're not here by accident. You were directed, and we both know who by. Charlie Anstey and Issy Kaufmann were in cahoots and looking after their own interests—which did not include yours, Bebbinger—this evening. That left only Lucinda Anstey to ride over to the Ackerman quartz mill and warn you that I'd be going to the sheriff concerning you before long. Trouble was, the silly girl clearly didn't know that Charlie and Issy were aiming to do away with me. It's a tangled skein, Bebbinger, and, if all had gone as those two intended, you'd have waited for me in vain; but chance has swung it your way. The devil surely looks after his own!'

'He's a good boss,' Bebbinger agreed. 'Have you killed Anstey and Kaufmann? Seems to me you must have done.'

'Didn't they need killing?'

'They did. By me.'

'You may still have your chance with Issy.'

'How's that?'

'Anstey's dead, but Issy's wounded.'

'Where is Kaufmann now?'

'I don't know. He escaped me. Around. Could be most anywhere.'

Bebbinger glanced about him involuntarily. 'I think you're telling the truth.'

'It is the truth,' Sam said. 'I'll swear Kaufmann is carrying lead where it weighs heavy. Why don't you take some of your boys and ride off and seek him? He can't be far away.'

'Leaving you here with only the lightest of guards?' Bebbinger queried disdainfully. 'You'll have to do better than that, Cade.'

'Some people will not be helped,' Sam sighed.

'There's no road you're going to get away,' Bebbinger said vindictively. 'Men who really cross me up don't die easily. I'm going to have some fun at your expense before long. There's also Big Alan Cooper's death to pay you out for. Yes, we found his body among the pines, with that knife stuck in it. His death had to be your doing, as we figured it out when certain information came to hand. Altogether, I reckon you deserve to die hard, Cade, and I've thought up how it's going to be.'

'Whatever happens in life,' Sam said, grunting like a hog, 'you have to take it from where it comes.'

'All right, all right,' Bebbinger said tolerantly. 'Have your laugh now. Mine will be the last laugh, the one that really counts. Come the dawn, Cade, I'm going to sit with my back against a tree and a mug of coffee in my hand, and watch you die about as slowly and painfully

as a man may die.' He paused, audibly suck-
ing the air into his lungs and stretching his legs
hard against the strings of his saddle. 'There's
too much yak here, Reed—and you, Crossman.
Tie Cade's hands behind his back and stuff a
gag in his mouth. Then we'll take him to the
Valley of the Ravens. If the legend be true,
hundreds of people have died there, and the
weird old place ought to perk up no end if we
spill new blood on its grass.'

Guns were cocked threateningly and, though
tempted to make a break for it, Sam realized
that such action would be suicidal. Thus he
could do nothing but sit rigid on his horse and
let the two outlaws who closed on him bind his
hands over his tailbone and tie a neckerchief
tightly into his mouth. The Valley of the
Ravens, eh? Well, it was not far away—not
much over a mile east of Hazewater. Legend
did indeed have it that the valley had been a
killing ground for the Utes, and Sam could only
pray that he was not going to go on the record
of the ages as the victim who had died there
most horribly of all. He would never give up
hope, but it was hard to stay brave in the face
of some things.

'Finished?' Bray Bebbinger demanded, as
Crossman and Reed began checking each
other's work.

'Yeah, he'll do,' one of the pair responded.

'Let's move out,' the gang leader command-ed. 'Lead his horse, Reed.'

The man who had just answered Bebbinger—thick-shouldered and bulky in the moonrays—caught up Sam's reins and began drawing the prisoner's mount behind his own as the gang started moving down the trail in the direction of Hazewater. Riding erect, despite his bonds, Sam kept his knees pressed firmly to his mount's sides in order to stay in place. The party clattered along at a fair speed for a few hundred yards but, on approaching the right-hand bend which carried the trail towards the town's boundary, Bebbinger did what Sam had been expecting and led off the beaten way and into the country on the left. After that, riding now at no better than a trot, the horsemen mov-ed into a shallow curve that bore them around the northern edge of Hazewater, along the shores of the lake just beyond the built up area, and on to the continuation of the trail which they had so recently left at the western end of the town. They followed this eastwards for about half a mile and then turned off to the right, passing through a cleft in a wall of stone and finally bearing left through a dying wood that stank of dry rot and entering a small valley which had vertical walls on its southern side and at its eastern end, while on its northern flank it sent terraces that were low and wide stepping back to a ridge which formed a regular line against the night sky. On the lower terraces, just visible now as wide-spreading blotches of darkness, were areas of woodland, and out of these came a faint, rasping protest from bird voices at this nocturnal disturbance. 'Hear them, Cade?' Bebbinger called back. 'Ravens. Thousands upon thousands of them. There's no raven on earth as foul-feeding and bloody-beaked as our Nevada raven. It won't be long before you meet them in their shrieking flocks. Then—heaven help you!'

Sam shuddered. There had been something in the gang boss's voice which had set the nerves prickling all over him. Now Bebbinger was giving vent to a low, devilish laughter. What exactly had the man got in mind. To judge from the cruelty in the sounds he made, it must be something quite awful.

They pursued a line down the middle of the valley, and stopped when they had covered about a third of its length. Bebbinger dismounted, and his men did likewise. Then the gang leader ordered Reed and Crossman to help Sam off his horse. This the two badmen did, none too gently, and they deposited the prisoner on the grass of the valley floor, where

106

he sat debating what his chances would be if he jacked himself erect while the gangsters were talking together and made a run for it, hands still tied behind his back and his breathing restricted by the tight gag about his mouth; but his wiser self knew that this piece of nonsense stood even smaller hopes of success than the break that he had contemplated when first captured. It still made no sense to get killed prematurely, and he remained motionless and waited anxiously for what Bebbinger would order next.

'Shovels!' the gang boss barked presently, digging his right heel into the ground at what appeared to be a soft spot. 'Dig here!'

There was a movement around the horses. Then two members of the gang—other than Reed and Crossman—stepped up with shovels in their hands and cut the sods away at the place where Bebbinger had indicated. Then they began to dig out the soil beneath, toiling away until they stood knee-deep in the ground, when they paused by tacit agreement and sleeved the sweat off their faces.

'Keep at it!' Bebbinger harried.

'This is hard work, Bray!' the bigger of the two diggers protested.

'Too bad!' Bebbinger jeered. 'I've let you boys get out of shape. Dig, damn you, dig!

You've got to go down another four feet yet.

'Make him do it,' the larger digger urged, nodding in Sam's direction. 'All this is for his benefit, ain't it?'

'I despair of you, Mallin!' the gang leader declared. 'You've got no bump of safety. A shovel in the hands of a desperate man is a mighty dangerous weapon. Get on with it!'

Mallin resumed digging, and so did his companion, but the second man could not forbear to say: 'Are Jockey Mallin and me the only working muscle in this outfit?'

'Aw, quit your grousing!' Bebbinger snapped. 'You're as bad as he is, Conway. I'll see you get a rest when you really need it.'

There was no more said. The labourers began to work rhythmically again. Fresh earth showered steadily onto the now considerable pile that was rising beside the deepening hole. Sam was still puzzled as he looked on, for he was no closer than before to deciding what the boss outlaw had in store for him. At first he had supposed that Mallin and Conway were going to dig his grave, but he had realized some time back that this excavation was hardly one undertaken for the sole purpose of receiving a corpse. His long frame certainly wouldn't lie flat in the bore-hole yonder.

Then somebody gave a sinister laugh and

108

said: 'Pity it ain't to be soldier ants.'

'Hear that, Bray?' another voice asked. 'Orville Fowler favours soldier ants.'

'No anthills around,' Bebbinger responded, 'Ravens are just as greedy, and they take bigger bites.'

Sam understood then. They were going to stand him upright in that hole and bury him from the neck down. After that they were going to use some method—undoubtedly bloody—of enticing the ravens to him; and the black birds would perhaps start on him accidentally—or even experimentally—first pecking the eyes out of his head, then stripping the flesh from his skull, and finally boring through to his brain. But he would, of course, be dead long before they got there. Very painfully and messily dead. Bray Bebbinger was certainly demonstrating a touch of sadistic genius here.

The diggers were changed at about the yard and a half mark. Bebbinger named Reed and Foster to take over on the shovels. The new pair worked with an energy which betrayed their desire to have the job over and done with, and they soon removed the rest of the soil that Bebbinger required dug out of the hole. Then the gang boss went forward and inspected the work—even to the extent of jumping down into the hole and measuring the base of his neck against the job done—and, having expressed his satisfaction, he scrambled out again and ordered Foster and Reed to pick the captive up and lower him feet-first into the excavation.

Sam gathered his legs as he watched the two men moving towards him. It was not so much that he was afflicted by a sudden loss of nerve as that he felt an angry desire to make a fight of it. But, before he could start kicking out, one of the pair—the bulky Reed, he thought— seemed to divine his intentions and clapped the barrel of a revolver against the side of his head. He lost consciousness instantly, and must have remained senseless for several minutes for, when he came back to himself, he was already in the hole and buried up to his waist. He tried with all his might to lift his body, but found that the soil already held him fast, and he could do nothing but moan softly to himself and watch the burial process continue until only his neck and head remained above the earth and the loose soil at the top of the hole had been stamped down tightly by heavy men with more than willing feet.

'Fair job,' Bebbinger acknowledged. 'Have you got that jackrabbit you caught this after- noon, Fowler?'

'Sure,' came the reply from the willowy six- footer on Sam's right who wore a particularly high-crowned J.B.

'I want you to get it,' the gang leader said. 'Hulk it, then spread the innards around Cade's head. Cut the carcass up as you like. You can throw the joints down in another ring. If I know those ravens, they'll be starving at first light, and a free meal will be just what the doctor ordered. Won't it, Cade?'

Sam tried to answer, but the gag was still about his mouth and no sound would come. Worse, he realised now that the blow from the gun barrel had somehow upset the rhythm of his breathing. Black panic enveloped him. His mind reeled, and blood rained behind his eyes. He was choking. If something wasn't done for him in a moment, he was going to lose—

CHAPTER SEVEN

Fortunately, Bebbinger detected Sam's plight and removed the gag as the three-parts buried man was about to lose consciousness again. Able now to draw in air through his mouth, Sam turned back his head and filled his lungs, aware after that of signals inside his body sorting themselves out and his chest starting to function normally again. But the panic remained, and he felt a terrible urge to scream; yet some instinct came to his rescue and suppressed the sound in his throat, for he knew that Bebbinger would soon gag him again if he made any real noise, and he felt he must avoid that at all costs.

The man named Fowler disappeared towards the horses about then. He returned a minute or so later with a big jackrabbit hanging from his left hand and a knife held in his right. There was still enough power in the moonlight for Sam to watch the crook gutting and jointing the dead animal. Then he smelled the new blood as the parts of the jackrabbit's anatomy were spread around his neck. 'How's that, Bray?' Fowler asked, as he finally stepped back from his foul task.

'Neither more nor less than I wanted,' Bebbinger answered. 'Okay, Orville. You can hang about here. Play guard—have a strut if you want. Just see to it that no coyote makes a meal here during the dark hours. It won't be dawn for a long time yet.'

'Okay,' Fowler said reluctantly. 'Sounds like you've got other plans.'

'For me and the rest, yes,' Bebbinger agreed. 'We're short on grub and such. Maybe we can rustle up some supplies in town. Could be there's a storekeeper still poking about. The breed appears never to sleep. I don't aim to break in anywhere. Not worth it in the circumstances. Anyhow, we'll have a try.'

'I don't reckon you'll buy much but a bottle of booze in Hazewater at this hour,' Fowler reflected. 'You wouldn't be planning a party by the lake?'

'And if I was?' Bebbinger inquired aggressively.

Fowler laughed shortly—fear in the sound—as if he were now trying to laugh the matter off. 'Mosquitoes. Big as humming birds.'

'You don't like 'em?'

'They bite, Bray—they bite.'

'Do they now?' Bebbinger sneered. 'There's always something. Tell you what, Orville. I'll personally undertake to make you a perfect world next time round.'

'This one's okay by me.'

'Remember that,' Bebbinger counselled, 'and you may stick around to enjoy it another year or two yet.'

Fowler cleared his throat, but had no more to say. Then Bebbinger and the four other members of his gang went to their horses and mounted up. Sam heard them ride out of the valley, but the visual aspect of their departure was lost on him, for locked into the earth as he was, he could only gaze in the opposite direction and a little to either side.

During the next few minutes Fowler kicked and shuffled in the vicinity of the three-parts buried man, muttering petulantly to himself at short intervals; then, apparently tiring of this light exercise and his own bad mood, he stopped near Sam and asked: 'What's it like, buried up in there?'

'Hot,' Sam answered; for hot it was. 'I feel like I'm burning up.'

'Don't die on me before sunrise.'

'Can't promise you anything.'

'Kid's game,' Fowler said contemptuously. 'Bray Bebbinger has got a touch of the spoiled boy about him. Me, I'd have put a bullet through your brain and left you for the ravens to pick.'

'That's what you'd have done,' Sam conceded. 'Quick and simple, and it comes out just the same. Have you got a drink of water about you, Fowler?'

'He'd lynch me!'

'He have to know?'

'Cade, Bray knows everything.'

Sam spat dirt out of his mouth. 'Some gift that. He sure is a caution, Orville.'

'You're a sight too familiar, Cade!' Fowler snorted. 'Can't talk to you. I'm off for a walk north of here.'

'I'd keep you company,' Sam said, 'but I've got a bootful.'

'You won't be so damned chipper soon,' Fowler rasped. 'If a coyote should come sniffin' around, bawl at it, and I'll be back like jerked lightning to do the honours.'

'Bless you, sir!'

'Huh,' Fowler grunted, and stalked off into a gloom that was thickening by degrees as the moon went on sailing across the sky.

With Fowler out of sight, Sam swallowed at the dryness of his mouth and throat, all too conscious that his bodily temperature was still rising apace from the lack of ventilation to his skin

115

and that he was dehydrating at a rate that life itself could not support for long. As the time dragged by, he suffered to an extent that increased proportionally with his decline in condition, and he seemed actually to have entered hell and to be a human cinder when, through his increasing daze, he heard voices nearby and one of them calling the contraction of his Christian name in familiar tones. 'Sam! Sam!'

Could it be uncle Bert? Certainly it was no member of the Bebbinger gang shouting his name, and he wasn't yet so far gone that the mistake could occur. 'Uncle Bert!' he croaked out.

'Over there,' somebody said tensely. 'Do I see horses?'

'Yes, you do,' another man confirmed.

Sam tried again, and this time his voice was both louder and clearer. 'Uncle Bert!'

And it was Bert Anstey's voice that said excitedly: 'He's here all right, Sheriff. Where are you, Sam?'

'Here!' Sam answered, his senses clearing completely now. 'Buried up to my neck! Can't see you! My eyes are looking the wrong way!'

A few moments later mounts stopped close to where Sam's head was jutting out of the valley floor, and he heard riders step down and hurry towards him. 'My dear, dear boy!' uncle

Bert exclaimed, kneeling amidst the dismembered portions of the jackrabbit, his hat appearing grotesquely large at the present set his head and his garments smelling of mothballs. 'What have they done to you?'

'Thank God it can still be undone!' Sam responded fervently. 'Dig me up, gents!'

'Holy Wars!' a gruff voice complained. 'We'll need a shovel. Get you back to the office and fetch one, Gabriel!'

'Sure thing, Sheriff,' a higher pitched male voice said obediently.

Sam knew then that both Sheriff Stockman and his deputy, Gabriel Lent, were present. With Uncle Bert there too, he felt in safe hands—though he had to warn them that Orville Fowler was still somewhere in the valley, and that Bebbinger and the balance of his gang were probably on the prowl in town— but none of it did much to help him as the deputy sheriff remounted and galloped off towards Hazewater, for his suffering had not abated and he believed that life itself would shortly slip from him unless he could get some liquid into his body. 'Water!' he gasped. 'I'm burning up! It's like standin' in a hot oven!'

'I've got water in my canteen,' the sheriff said. 'Start digging him out with your hands, Anstey. We've got to get air to his skin.'

'Some job!' uncle Bert observed, clawing out the dirt that had been packed in under his nephew's jaw.

The sheriff brought his canteen. Uncorking it, he nudged Bert Anstey aside and knelt next to Sam, putting the neck of the container to Sam's mouth and letting the entrapped man drink his fill. Then, corking the canteen again, he laid it aside and added his two hands to the pair with which Bert Anstey had resumed toiling away. Their work soon made a difference. Sam began to live more comfortably. And before long, because the soil lower down had had no chance to consolidate, they were able to do more still, their efforts clearing a space about Sam's chest and waist that entirely relieved his suffering. 'I thank you,' he said. 'Much obliged; and if I can have another pull at that waterbottle, I'll be even more so.'

Again the square-jawed Sheriff Stockman helped Sam to a drink. 'We'll soon have you right out of there,' the lawman said, 'once we have the shovel. What was the purpose of burying you like this?'

Sam explained about the ravens. 'Bray Bebbinger intended that they should have my head for breakfast come sunup.'

'The cruel villain!' Bert Anstey roared.

'He's all of that,' Sam agreed. 'Figures you

must have had some talk with Lucinda. I don't
see how you could be here otherwise.'

'I had a talk with her all right,' Bert Anstey
said grimly. 'Sheriff Stockman knows about it.
I had to tell him everything in order to get him
here to help you.'

'Go on,' Sam said.

Uncle Bert told how Issy Kaufmann, on his
knees and dying, had crawled into the Anstey
cottage earlier that night and, in his near-
delirium, babbled to Lucinda—with whom he
had lately professed to be in love—how, keeping time with her brother Charlie's departure
for California, he and Charlie had planned
to lure Sam Cade to a remote cave out Ute
Canyon way, where they had stashed some gold
belonging to Cade, and there murder him.
Only, as Issy had related it, the would-be
killers had bungled the job and both got shot.
Before Kaufmann died, he had pleaded with
Lucinda—who had, without Issy's knowledge,
already been in contact with Bebbinger that
evening and arranged with Bray to waylay Sam
as he returned from the Ute Canyon area and
later kill him slowly in the Valley of the
Ravens—to see that Bebbinger avenged his
death on Sam, and she had promised that she
would. 'All this didn't come out in quite such
good order as I've made it sound,' Bert Anstey

119

concluded, 'and I was so bewildered by it all that it took me a while to sort it out and decide what I was going to do; but once I'd made up my mind, I shook that daughter of mine until she provided what details were lacking, then made for the law office as fast as I could go. Thank God we got here before any real harm had come to you, Sam!'

'Amen,' Sam agreed fervently. 'Sounds to me like it could've worked out an awful lot worse.'

'I can already think of the first thirty five questions that I want answered,' Stockman said sourly. 'It's complicated.'

'No, it ain't,' Sam assured him; 'it's simple as can be. But it does seem to me that you may not have heard that Bray Bebbinger and his gang have been hiding out to the northwest of here in the abandoned Ackerman quartz mill. You'll want to posse up, I reckon, come dawn, and gallop over there. Because it's plain to me that's where Bray and company will be riding back when they leave town tonight—which they may already have done, since it's a safe bet that my guard, Orville Fowler, long ago saw and worked out what's happening here and has high-tailed for where his boss can be found with his story.'

'Why is it plain to you?' Stockman asked.

'They'll be going back for their loot,' Sam replied. 'I saw no sign anybody in the gang was carrying anything of the sort tonight.'

'I see,' Stockman growled. 'Sounds to me like I'll have to take a posse out. But I'm no man to follow another's mind where the responsibility is mine. No, dammit, I'm not! Howsoever, it's going to take me a day to get all this sorted through and clear in my head, so I'll have to act where the need's obvious and it's clear in another's.'

'You'll regret it if you don't,' Sam assured him.

'How did I come to take up law work?' Stockman complained. 'Its work, work, work, and nothing to show for it.'

'You've got me,' Sam pointed out modestly.

'Sam,' said uncle Bert in his gravest voice, 'there's something I've got to ask you. It's about Charlie. Issy Kaufmann said my boy had been shot. Is he still—alive?'

Sam shook his head. 'I'm sorry, uncle Bert. The slug that killed Charlie came from Issy Kaufmann's gun, but I guess he wouldn't have stopped it if I hadn't pulled him in the way of it while protecting myself.'

'I expect you did what you felt you had to do,' Bert Anstey said heavily.

'It was how I did it or nothing, Uncle Bert.'

'I always knew he'd come to a bad end,' the other sighed. 'It's going to break his poor mother's heart.'

'It gets worse,' Stockman gritted. 'Now we've got another dead man.' He put his right hand on his gun as hoofbeats echoed to them from the way into the Valley of the Ravens. 'That sounds like my man Lent coming back.'

The rider did indeed prove to be Gabriel Lent, and the deputy handed Stockman the shovel for which he had been sent. The sheriff passed the shovel to Bert Anstey, and for several minutes after that there was a lot of digging done around Sam's lower body; and then, with the bulk of the earth removed, the three men put their arms about the figure standing in the hole and lifted him bodily out of the clinging soil, placing him on the grass of the valley bottom, where he lay gently pumping his legs and otherwise easing the circulation in his stiffened body.

'You'll be all right now, Cade,' the sheriff observed. 'I'll leave my deputy and your uncle to look after you while I go and do what's needful.'

'What's that, Jack?' Gabriel Lent asked in surprise. 'Where are you off to?'

'Just into town,' Stockman replied. 'I'm going to get a few of our old faithfuls out of bed and form a posse. Cade tells me Bray Bebbinger has been using the Ackerman quartz mill as a hideout while working in these parts. I aim to ride over to the mill and see if we can't catch them while they're stowing their loot. Failing that, we may be able to pick up their trail beyond the hideout and hunt them down.'

'It'll be dawn before you get started,' Lent observed.

'Before *we* get started,' Stockman emphasized. 'I'll call on you when we get back home, Cade. I imagine you will be staying at your uncle's.'

'No, I won't,' Sam said, easing himself erect and limping back and forth across the nearby ground. 'I'm going to ride with you and that posse of yours.'

'Are you crazy?' the sheriff inquired. 'After what you've been put through tonight? I'd never encourage any man to pamper himself, but there are limits to what he should allow himself to suffer. I reckon you need a rest, Cade. A good long rest. You'd likely be a drag on the posse anyhow.'

'Talk so damned silly!' Sam snorted. 'I'm still sound in wind and limb. Know anybody who has a better right to ride with you, Sheriff?'

'I guess not,' Stockman admitted, striding

to his horse, swinging up cleanly, and then wheeling his mount away. 'I'm not your nurse. Come if you want.'

Followed by his uncle and Gabriel Lent, Sam began searching for his horse. He found it standing quite close by. Opening up the saddle-bag on the beast's near side, he took out his gunbelt and gazed at it distastefully. It was, he supposed, time that he strapped the thing on. He hadn't been able to avoid killing up to now, and he was sure that he wouldn't be able to after this.

CHAPTER EIGHT

The posse left Hazewater during the hour after dawn. It numbered eighteen men, including Sheriff Jack Stockman and his deputy, Gabriel Lent. Sam was there, riding unobtrusively at the centre of the party, and beside him, on an ageing grey mare, sat his grieving uncle Bert who, after taking home the black news concerning his son Charlie, had returned to the law office yard and asked permission of Stockman to join the posse, explaining that, as Bray Bebbinger appeared to have encouraged his son and daughter into evil ways, he would like to have a hand in making the gang boss pay for it. Stockman had agreed to the request and, though Sam had argued that his uncle was too old and lacked the physical fitness for posse work—Bert Anstey earned his living as the typesetter on the Hazewater 'Bulletin'—the lawman had shrugged off the protest and reminded Sam that Anstey was original pioneer stock and could still be relied upon when the going got tough, and that had ended the matter.

Led by Stockman and Gabriel Lent, the posse was soon three miles clear of Hazewater and into desert country. Indeed the party covered virtually the same ground as Sam had travelled when tracking cousin Charlie and Issy Kaufmann to the Ackerman quartz mill. The only real difference in anything between then and now was the matter of the temperature. Then Sam had sweltered, but now he shivered. The morning was remarkably cool for the place and time of year, and a pearly mist clung to the rocks and hung just above the ground, its chilling fingers creeping through cotton garments and raising goose bumps on the flesh beneath. Perhaps because of the clear skies above it and the unhindered coming of the sun, this condensation grew thicker as the posse approached the foothills of the Trinity Mountains and was only just starting to dissolve when the law party arrived at the foot of the quartz mill's approach road and began climbing cautiously through the vapours that threaded the pinewood towards the plateau above on which the Ackerman's buildings stood.

Like the rest of the possemen, Sam was tense and kept his hand near his gun; but the birds sang in the trees and everywhere was still. The climb through the approach road's left-hand bend went on slowly, and then, clearing the mist, the posse topped out at the edge of the plateau and saw the quartz mill before them. There was still no movement anywhere, and no challenge. All present began to relax, for there was no longer much doubt that the Ackerman was deserted.

Stockman called a halt in front of the mill itself. Then, after ordering everybody else to remain on their horses, he dismounted himself and walked into the building through its main door and vanished, re-appearing about two minutes later at the office window on the right of the entrance and calling through the glass: 'Nobody here now, but there are plenty of signs that men were around not long ago. Look for tracks, Gabriel. Search around the northern edge of the hilltop first.'

The deputy sheriff left the posse and moved into the northern quarter of the mill site. Dismounting, still in sight of Sam and the rest, he cast about him for sign, and was almost immediately successful, for he had not covered more than twenty yards to his left when his face came round, its slightly pop-eyed features showing excitement, and he shouted. 'Several horses went down this here slope not two hours ago! There's still moisture where a sod was raised!'

Stockman had just emerged from the mill,

and been in time to hear this news. Looking among the faces of the riders seated above him, he picked out Sam's and said: 'I think you read it right, Cade.'

'Never did know a badman to leave his loot behind,' Sam reflected. 'Seems Bebbinger is no different from the rest.'

'In that respect,' Stockman acknowledged, returning to his horse and stepping into leather again. 'Let's go!'

They rode across the plateau and joined Gabriel Lent, who was back in his saddle and waiting for them. Then, with Stockman and his deputy again in the lead, they passed over the northern edge of the hilltop and moved down the fairly steep gradient beyond, coming at the foot of the descent to a stretch of flat, stony ground where a thin covering of dust carried the trace of the men who had ridden this way ahead of them with enough clarity for steady progress to be maintained in pursuit.

The sun was fully risen by now and the light low upon the land. Every colour met the eye in perfect hue, and the sky was bright blue and cloudless over all. About the posse distance fled to one yard short of infinity, and it seemed to Sam that men and horses shrank to little or nothing against this awesome panorama that gradually took in fields of alkali, suncracked gulches and arroyos, rocklands and ponds of lye-water, and clay slopes that bore discoloured firetops—reds and yellows and bronzes—up to the soaring ironstone cliffs that formed the footstools of the Trinity peaks that lined the west.

Moving between these slopes and the pools of lye-water, the posse stayed with the ever-present sign and rode northwards through the gathering heat of the day and, as monotony crept into the ride, several of the horsemen acknowledged their disturbed night and bowed their heads, almost nodding off in their seats. It would undoubtedly have reduced the boredom of the chase if some glimpse, however, distant, had been caught of the quarry, but never once were the outlaws glimpsed ahead. By the end of the morning, Sam heard remarks being made to the effect that the posse was no longer all that far away from the town of Lovelock, and the possemen of the more experienced kind began to ask one another what Bebbinger could possibly have in mind, for the country beyond Lovelock and out towards Mount Imlay was largely desert and uninhabited. In other words, it could be of little interest to hold-up men who worked the roads, and several vague theories were advanced on the general theme of lying low, but nobody seemed to take that facet of the talk very seriously and Sam found himself growing uneasy because of it.

This pursuit was altogether too straightforward for his liking, and he could not believe that this was because Bray Bebbinger had not anticipated being followed out to the Ackerman quartz mill and then hunted by the Hazewater law thereafter. Bebbinger had the kind of crafty mind that never stopped thinking, and he would have realized from the outset that the pursuers would be too close behind his gang to permit choosing an escape route in rocky highlands where his trail would soon be lost. When you stopped to consider it fully, Bebbinger's best ploy must be to draw his hunters deep into the wilderness, lulling them all the time, and then turn on them and inflict the kind of casualities that would destroy the posse's will to follow. Obviously that meant an ambush and, as the law party was now not too far from a settlement, that ambush could no longer be too much delayed; so, when you saw a battlemented ridge of sandstone like the one now visible ahead sitting across your path, you had to look at it and wonder, for it would be hard to imagine a better hiding place from which to round on an enemy.

Uncle Bert hadn't been exactly talkative during the ride—and Sam had been careful to respect the reasons for the older man's silence and leave him alone—but now he raised Anstey from his brown study and gave his uncle the benefit of his recent thinking, asking the other's opinion, and uncle Bert said that Sam ought to put the possibilities to Jack Stockman without delay; so Sam cupped a hand about his mouth and called: 'Hey, Sheriff!'

Stockman craned out of the posse's lead. 'Cade?'

'A word in your ear?'

'Ride up and join me.'

Sam manoeuvred his horse clear of those which hemmed in his own, then cantered down the right-hand wing of the party and turned in at the sheriff's elbow. Given permission to speak, he said the same things to Stockman that he had said to his uncle and, when he had finished, got the idea that the sheriff had not been too much impressed, for they had covered a further hundred yards in silence before the lawman remarked that he couldn't call Sam a fool.

'Why not?' Sam inquired, disconcerted.

'Because that would be plain asking for it,' Stockman admitted. 'I've had thoughts along the same lines myself, and there's no denying that ridge is a prime place for an ambush. All the same, though, there are other things that

Bebbinger may have taken into consideration.'

'Such as?'

'He knows a town sheriff's jurisdiction is limited,' Stockman replied, 'and I'm already out of mine. I ought to have ordered this posse to face about half an hour ago.'

'So—why didn't you?'

'Those guys back there are volunteers on their own time,' the sheriff explained. 'I have to consider their feelings in a situation like this. They don't like having their time wasted, and I may need their help another day. Regardless of rules and regulations, I've got to hold a balance between the sense of doing my job and the nonsense of not.'

'I guess you have at that,' Sam conceded, feeling a sudden respect for this man whom he had previously regarded as a no-account time-server. 'What else about Bebbinger?'

'He's not wanted for murder,' Stockman answered. 'Oh, I haven't the faintest doubt he's a string of killings behind him, but the law doesn't yet want him on a capital charge. If the reports are all to be credited, Bebbinger has got his head screwed on right. It's my candid opinion, therefore, that he won't make life harder for himself than it has to be and will think twice before shooting up a posse. Murder would make him the subject of special attention from the Federal Law, and he wouldn't want to have the riding marshals after him.'

'Makes sense,' Sam admitted. 'Okay, Sheriff. I've said my piece. You're in charge.'

Stockman nodded absently, and murmured a word of thanks. Moving out to his right, Sam slowed his horse almost to a stop and dropped back down the side of the posse, rejoining his uncle and quickly telling the other what had passed up front. Bert Anstey agreed that the sheriff had made a couple of good points with regard to Bebbinger—though, like his nephew, he was not wholly convinced that Stockman was right—then lapsed into silence again, leaving Sam to gaze rather fixedly at the ridge of sandstone which loomed before them as a barrier of ever-increasing magnitude.

The alkali dust smoked up, whitening the possemen, and the sweat-stained horses trotted onwards, already blowing tiredly. Always the tracks left by the outlaws went on before them. Through rock-piles and outcrops they passed, the sunrays slanting hotly above them in the lows and burning straight into their faces on the higher land, and then, still invested by the debris of Time, they entered the shadow of the ridge itself and were nearing the base of the red sand gradient which cushioned the weirdly eroded stone above, when a shout went up at the head of the posse and all the riders present jerked to a halt. 'They're about here somewhere!' Stockman shouted at the top of his voice. 'The tracks have ceased ahead of us!'

Startled—though far from surprised—Sam stood up in his stirrups and twisted round, using his extra height to look over the heads about him and peer among the heaped rocks and spurs of the neighbourhood for a first sight of the gangsters, realizing that the ambush which he knew was about to manifest was to be an even smarter one than he had expected, since the outlaws had clearly let the law party ride past their places of concealment with the intention of firing on the possemen from the rear; and that was what happened now, for the badmen suddenly lifted into view on the left with their rifles at their shoulders and began shooting into the posse from a range of no more than thirty yards.

Two saddles emptied immediately, and there were cries of pain as other men were hit. Within two seconds another volley ripped through the posse. Three more riders tumbled to the ground. Horses, reared, or swung to left or right, cannoning into each other. Chaos reigned. Bullets hummed. The six rifles back there cracked and boomed. Sam kicked his horse clear of the confusion. He looked around for

Jack Stockman, expecting the sheriff to start issuing orders of some kind, but he saw almost at once that Stockman had been hit and collapsed helplessly over his mount's neck. Gabriel Lent, the deputy sheriff, was still unharmed, but shock had clearly paralysed his never remarkable wits, and Sam perceived that a massacre was in the offing if something drastic was not done to check the rifle fire.

Snatching out his pistol, he rode forward and then to his left, shouting: 'Follow me! Charge 'em! Come on! They ain't got us beat yet!'

Sam feared that, for all the inspiration that he was attempting to spread about him, he would get no response; but uncle Bert was among the few at the heart of the posse who had kept their nerve and wits; and, as Anstey fetched round, the others followed him, and the men made up a body of four or five horsemen in Sam's wake.

They went straight for the riflemen among the rocks and, spreading out now, began shooting. Sam felt the whip of a bullet as it scored the front of his saddle, and looked towards the outlaw who had fired the shot, seeing a tall, thin, hardbitten fellow—Orville Fowler, he was pretty sure—and, as the other took aim at him again, shot at him off an extended arm. The bullet went in dead centre, blood springing into the front of the villain's shirt, and then the man toppled backwards and raised a fountain of dust as he hit the earth. Sam's horse lunged onwards, hooves showering rubble among the boulders, and now its rider saw an ugly face, tanned and square—with a tobacco-stained mouth and wall-eye—looking at him over the sights of a Winchester. The rifle exploded within six feet of Sam's head, and he felt the slug almost literally part his hair but, though he triggered an instant reply, the out-law's face vanished ahead of his bullet, drilled through at the middle of the forehead. Sam slanted a glance to his left, but who had fired the killing shot he couldn't tell, and it mattered not at all.

Jinking to either hand, Sam went for other targets, his pistol jetting through the palls of gunsmoke that were now drifting among the combatants, and he saw a third badman go down. But, demoralised by the abrupt change in their fortunes, the surviving gansters had plainly had enough, for they faced about after the fall of their third comrade and ran for a group of large rocks situated a few yards to the west of them, where their horses were waiting. Tipping their rifles into their saddleholsters, the three badmen still active—Bebbinger promi-nent among them—mounted up and spurred off across the land over which they and the posse had previously come, riding like men in fear of the devil.

Sam sent his mount surging after the trio. Middling their tracks, he fired a shot after the gang boss. Bray Bebbinger ducked, as from a near miss, and then his face twisted round, fiendishly flared at the mouth and eyes, and a moment later his Colt flashed a reply at the pursuer. Sam had not thought of being hit, and wasn't, but his horse jerked together as if it had run into a stone wall and dropped onto its belly, the impact pitching him out of his saddle and through a series of somersaults which all but robbed him of his senses and left him lying on his face in the shadow of a boulder that stood above him like a tombstone.

He tried to stir, but found that he could not, and a full minute went by before he could persuade his body to again start behaving in something like a normal manner. He needed helping hands to get him back on his feet, but none came and, finally, drawing on the whole of his will, he managed to struggle erect once more and reeled groggily to where his pistol lay, picking the weapon up and holstering it. Then he lurched back to his horse and looked down at the brute through pulsing cycles of vertigo, perceiving that Bebbinger's bullet had pierced its brain and that it was now food for the buzzards.

Feeling as if he were all fingers and thumbs, Sam removed his saddle, bridle, and bags from the dead brute; then, clumsily burdened, plodded back to the area in which most of the shooting had been done. He saw bodies lying at several points, and Deputy Sheriff Gabriel Lent was flapping around like an old hen and trying to stamp his authority on what was happening; but, fortunately, most of the surviving possemen were in full possession of their wits and some kind of order was already emerging from the chaos which the fighting had left.

A very sorry-looking Jack Stockman was sitting on a rock and receiving attention for his right collar-bone which had been shot through; and, while Sam paused to make sure that the sheriff's life was in no danger, he had no doubts about where his first duty lay, for Bert Anstey was no longer in his saddle or moving among the possemen who were on their feet. The realization was disquieting in itself, and the still partially bemused Sam began walking the area in a state of mounting agitation and it was with great relief that he found his uncle sitting propped between two nestling rocks and examining a wound high on the left side of his waist that looked bloody and painful but far from mortal. Nevertheless the shock of the wound and the older man's far from first class physical condition had to be borne in mind, and Sam handled uncle Bert very carefully as he plugged and bound the injury with strips torn off the tail of his relation's shirt, then moved Anstey into the shade of an outcrop and left him with a half-filled waterbottle in his lap.

Now Sam turned his attention to doing whatever he could elsewhere, and he soon discovered that the posse had been truly savaged with three men dead and five others wounded—two of them rather seriously.

'It's a shambles,' Sheriff Stockman admitted, his hurt shoulder now bandaged and his right arm supported by a high-angled sling. 'I should have taken more notice of you, Cade.'

'It could as easily have been you right and me wrong,' Sam responded. 'But did either of us expect to get cut up from the rear?'

'Anyhow, it's done,' Stockman said with a weighty finality. 'Bebbinger will pay.'

'He'll pay all right,' Sam agreed, tight-mouthed. Stockman rose from the boulder on which he had still been seated, wincing with pain. 'We have now to decide on what to do for the best. Our injured need a doctor, and the dead an undertaker. We could seek help in Lovelock, but I know for a fact there's no doctor there and the cemetery is the nearest piece of soft ground. I don't care where them outlaws lie, but our townsmen have the right to be buried where loved ones can visit their graves. Lovelock's ten miles away, and Hazewater more than thirty. Which is sayin', Cade, there's rest and sustenance nearby, while the ride home is long and must be hard on man and beast. So what's it to be? Am I to be democratic and ask all concerned for a vote on it?—or do I tell 'em what I want?'

'Do you figure what you want's right?' Sam asked.

'I do.'

'Like I said before, you're in charge here.'

Stockman nodded. 'We're going home.' And he gave notice of his decision in the loudest voice he could, asking those capable of it to catch the dispersed horses, then help the wounded astride and load up the dead.

Withdrawing from the small area in which most of the activity began taking place, Sam located and caught his uncle's horse, then led the creature back to where Bert Anstey sat and soon had the older man erect and into the saddle. After that—having made sure that his uncle was capable of controlling the horse and otherwise looking after himself in reasonable safety—Sam walked to the group of big rocks where the outlaws had stood their horses and helped himself to the best looking brute still present, leading it then to the rock beside which his saddle and other items were lying. Then, quickly undressing his appropriated mount, Sam strapped his own gear to its back and stepped up, giving the horse a slow turn or two along the base of the nearby sandstone ridge in order to ascertain its general responses and level of obedience. Satisfied that the animal was adequate to his needs, he returned to his uncle's side just as the surviving members of the posse—with the wounded prepared for the ride home and the dead face down over their saddles —were awaiting the signal to move out, and that was given within moments by Gabriel Lent on Jack Stockman's behalf.

The party soon put the ambush ground behind them. Through the noontide heat they slogged and into the afternoon. Progress could not be all that rapid—and periods of rest had to be taken for the benefit of the wounded and the horses—but the forward movement was otherwise smooth enough and by the middle of the evening they came again to the plateau on which the abandoned quartz mill stood.

Here they took a longer rest—for the horses were flagging badly now—but, though at this stage they could have sent to Hazewater for a waggon and help of the general sort to be despatched to them, it was the will of all present to continue, and before long they went on again, re-entering Hazewater just before one a.m. and starting to break up in a state of fatigue that was in some cases so profound that the men hardly knew what they were doing. 'Reckon we're all going to have to do the best we can where Doc Witton's services are concerned,' Sheriff Stockman announced in front of the law office—to as many men as were still present to hear. 'Those in need will just have to send their people around seeking him out. Let it be as the spirit moves it, folks, and no complaints, eh?'

Obviously, it was the only arrangement possible in the circumstances, with so much work for the doctor on hand, and Sam bore it in mind as he steered uncle Bert to the Anstey home and then got the older man indoors and onto the stairs, his tongue getting a trifle waspish as a lamp-bearing aunt Kathy and an hysterical Lucinda tacked on at his back, both firing questions at him so fast that he could not possibly give them adequate answers.

Watched by the two women, Sam undressed his uncle and got him to bed, and was more concerned than he let on when he saw that Bert Anstey's wound was still seeping blood and that his relation was extremely weak. Yet he supposed that, when his uncle's age and the length of the ride which he had just endured were taken into consideration, Bert Anstey had done well, and his voice was cheerful enough as he glanced round at the two women and said: 'Don't fret. He's almost as tough as I am. We'll do what we can for him by ourselves for now. Our posse took casualities, and doc's goin' to be a busy man tonight.'

'What's that an excuse for, Sam?' aunt Kathy demanded. 'Your uncle must have the attention he both needs and deserves.'

'I guess you're right about that,' Sam sighed. 'Okay. You'd better send Lucinda to Witton's house. I reckon Witton's wife will tell her where doc went first. After that she can do the round until she finds him.'

'Off you go, Lucinda!' her mother ordered sharply; and, momentarily looking daggers at Sam, the girl left the bedroom and went running down the stairs.

'I'm all right, Sam,' uncle Bert said from his bed. 'It was one hell of a day, but—I'm all right.'

'You're a brave old body,' Sam said sincerely. 'If you hadn't followed up when I shouted for the charge, those outlaws would've wiped Jack Stockman's posse out.'

143

'You're a good boy, Sam,' Bert Anstey assured him.

'There's Charlie,' Sam said, remembering.

'Your aunt and I would like you to know we don't hold that against you.'

'I take that kindly,' Sam said, looking more closely at his uncle's wound. 'Reckon you were a mite lucky, Uncle Bert. A bit higher up the body and you'd have lost a kidney.'

'There you are, mother,' Anstey said. 'All of a sudden we've got a medic in the family. We'll have him hanging out a shingle next.'

But aunt Kathy was not interested in the joke. She was weeping quietly, and had been since just after the mention of her son's name.

Sam felt empty inside, yet also on the defensive, for these could not be his aunt's first tears. 'Charlie had his chance,' he pleaded. 'The best one I could give him. He simply wasn't to be— You couldn't trust him, Aunt Kathy!'

'I know,' the woman said. 'But it's the black sheep that a mother has to think of first, Sam.'

'Is our girl so much better?' uncle Bert asked.

'There's no harm in her,' aunt Kathy retorted. 'She likes to show off. Maybe she's a *bit* wayward. But poor Charlie was weak and easily led. He didn't know how to keep out of trouble.'

'Lucinda does,' Bert Anstey commented. 'She makes trouble, then steps back from it, leaving somebody else to fight the fight.'

'Lucinda would never do a mean thing!' aunt Kathy defended. 'I won't listen to such words, Bert!'

' 'Twas she who warned Bray Bebbinger that he was in danger from me and the law,' Sam reflected.

'You can't prove it,' Kathy Anstey said defiantly.

'I suppose I can't,' Sam admitted. 'I reckon they'd call it circumstantial evidence in a court of law.'

'Anyway, she's my daughter,' said the man on the bed, 'and I don't much like her walking the town at this hour.'

'She'll soon be home,' Sam said.

'That she will,' Aunt Kathy said brokenly. 'Sam, I want my boy home too.'

'Tomorrow,' Sam promised. 'It's my job. You shall have your boy home tomorrow, Auntie. Now—will you set that lamp down on the chest-of-drawers and do something for uncle Bert?'

'What?'

'Boil some hot water. Then bring it to me in a basin, with a sponge, and I'll clean his wound. After that we can bandage him up

145

again—if Doc Witton hasn't already got here.'

Nodding, aunt Kathy placed the lamp on top of the chest-of-drawers that stood to the right of the bed and left the room, walking downstairs in what sounded like a renewed state of grief.

Sam sighed inwardly. Why were the innocent made to feel like the guilty?

CHAPTER NINE

The morning was still young when Sam put his horse to climbing the trail that led to the high country of the Ute Canyon area and the slope in which was situated the cave that held his gold and the mortal remains of cousin Charlie.

Yawning, Sam kept telling himself that it was great just to be alive, but his chest ached horribly and every joint in his body seemed to have had lead built into it overnight. On top of that, he could hardly keep his eyes open and felt downright weak. Admittedly, he had spent what portion of the night that he could call his own on his aunt Kathy's sofa in the parlour, and that ancient piece of horsehair furniture was hardly up to resting a man of his inches; but, when those factors had been evaluated and placed where they belonged, he still felt that something vital had gone out of him during the hours of darkness and wondered whether his condition this morning was what it felt like to be old.

Of course the coffee that cousin Lucinda had

made for him at breakfast could be partly responsible for the state of his health, as indeed could the eggs that she had boiled. But then, Lucinda's coffee had always been poisonous and she had never known a rotten egg from a good one. That she hated him very thoroughly for Charlie's death—as well as those womanly reasons of her own—he could not doubt, and he would not be surprised if she had spent that hour and more last night—which she claimed had been given up to locating the doctor—in chanting at the moon and weaving evil spells about his name; for, knowing what she was like when brooding on the catalogue of wrongs that she imagined to have been done her, he could believe her capable of any wickedness that might accelerate his journey towards the cemetery. But maybe he was doing her a slight wrong in supposing that she might have brought him harm through the stomach or by magical means, since she had once told him that only an axe in the head could be a fitting death for him; so perhaps he had better look to his rear when he returned to the cottage with her brother's body.

Sam kept riding and, though his suffering remained, the miles slipped by quickly enough and he was soon gazing once more—though in sunlight now which sharpened the raw details of the terrain—across the vast slope to the north of him that contained the cave to which he was going back; and presently he saw the con-siderable clump of manzanita which masked the bay off which the cavern opened and picked the spot ahead at which he would turn to his right and then ride down the declining land.

A vulture croaked overhead. The bird's shadow momentarily brushed Sam's face. He doubted that the creature's interest in him was a friendly one, and slanted a threatening eye skywards. The vulture stood on its left pinion and banked away to the south. It left an empty field of blue behind it. Everything seemed perfect again, and the cactuses under the ridges to the west were still in a riot of flower, yet the day had an ill-omened feeling about it. Sam could not define what was amiss, but it was there all the same.

He reached the selected spot. Now, touching right rein, he fetched his appropriated horse onto the slope adjacent. Keeping his movement slow and easy, he angled towards the clump of manzanita and arrived at the base of it a minute or two later. Then, still filled with uneasiness, he cast a long, slow look about him, but there appeared to be no living thing upon the earth nearby. Strangely influenced by the loneliness of the place, and wondering if what he felt could be fear, Sam dismounted. He ground-tied his horse, and made an effort to shake off his apprehension, telling himself that there was nothing here that he need fear. After that he turned to the vegetation and breasted into the bay beyond—where, obedient to its late master's memory, Charlie Anstey's mount still stood.

Standing beside the horse for a moment, Sam patted its neck. Directly ahead of him, the light filtering through the canopy of manzanita above now revealed the mouth of the cave to him quite plainly. He passed into the cave and bringing out a match, flicked fire with his thumbnail, raising his tiny light and wondering why he had heard nothing of the mules yet; and then, his matchfire playing across dead Charlie's frozen grin, he perceived the reason why—for the animals simply were not there.

It was a facer, and the shock of it took Sam's breath away. He dropped the match at his feet, and its light spluttered out, leaving him in the darkness, gasping and indecisive. The three mules could have strayed out onto the slope; there had been nothing to stop them—and they certainly lacked the long-suffering obedience of the more intelligent horse, as witness the continuing presence of Charlie Anstey's mount, unfed and unwatered for the better part of two days. Yes, the mules could have left the cave in search of graze; but he couldn't really believe it. He knew that they had been well-fed up to the time, which really couldn't be so long back, when they had finished their pile of fodder. No, the three brutes had been led out of here, and Sam was pretty sure that human hands had again been laid on his property. He must assume that he had been robbed for the second time.'

Putting a hand into his pocket, Sam took out and struck another match, this time carrying the flame to the ledge at the back of the cave on which the candle stood in its own grease. He touched off the wick, filling the cave with a much stronger glow than had been present a few moments ago, and now he studied the details of the gloomy scene about him with far more care than he had done previously.

He sought traces of human activity other than those which had originated with his late cousin Charlie and himself, but there was nothing present that offered the smallest clue as to who it was that had been here in his absence and led the three mules away. Nor, within the span of the last twenty-four hours, could he say with any degree of certainty when it had actually happened, and the possibilities in both cases were also difficult to assess, for

151

he reckoned that, of all the people involved who were left alive from yesterday, only cousin Lucinda could have known where his gold was, and she through learning it from her brother Charlie the day before yesterday.

The finger must point at Lucinda. Yet Sam could not credit that the girl had actually come to this remote cavern with the intention of robbing him. He felt sure that the presence of her brother's body would have deterred her from doing that, and he also could not believe that she possessed the sheer strength of mind necessary to putting that kind of revenge into effect.

Altogether, he was reasonably certain that he could see what had really happened. Last night, while she had been walking around Hazewater in search of the busy Doctor Witton, Lucinda had encountered Bray Bebbinger—who must have come straight back to this area after escaping the posse, most probably with the intention of squaring accounts with Sam—and told him that his enemy was indoors just now and hard to get at, but had suggested that the best and safest way of reaching a conclusion with Cade would be to steal his gold from his hiding place and then ambush him with a rifle when he started following up. The plan was crafty and compelling enough to be sure, yet also rather obvious—and Bebbinger must have realized that his enemy could hardly fail to see through it—but the gang boss would also have realized by now that Sam was no coward in the face of a challenge and would be ready to fight in whatever circumstances finally manifested, regardless of what Bebbinger must have perceived as his Ace-in-the-Hole—the fact that he still had two of his gangsters alive to help him make an uneven fight of it. Viewed with a cold eye, the outlaw leader must be figuring himself real clever and on a sure thing.

Sam scowled to himself. He was fed up with being everybody's bunny. He knew that he ought to be feeling at least wary—and maybe scared—but in fact he felt warlike. If that was how Bebbinger wanted to play it—okay. Let the villains exercise their wiles, and he would do the same. Accepting that they were three to his one, they would nevertheless find themselves with the more static part—while he would be free to scuttle around as he wished and surprise them whenever he could. Like that he would perhaps be able to eliminate the varmints one at a time. He felt grimly confident, and even a little excited. The events of the last two days had stirred him up no end. Bebbinger had better watch out. It was going to finish up as the biter bit!

But then—without the slightest warning—

the world rumbled and shook. A great force picked Sam up and hurled him against the rear wall of the cave; and it occurred to him, as his mind began folding into darkness, that an explosion had taken place at the mouth of the cave and that it had never been intended that he should pursue the gang boss. Instead it had been planned that he should lie entombed for ever at Charlie Anstey's side. Lucinda and Bebbinger had proved even smarter and more vindictive than he had expected. Then the blackness enfolded him totally and he lay in cold silence.

Yet, if for a moment death had him in its grip, it soon lost its hold on him again, for it was not long before he found himself struggling back from the dark emptiness and swearing aloud to himself with all the familiar fluency of Sam Cade. It was true that he could not see a thing, and that his mouth and nostrils were full of dust, but he could feel the hardness of the rock on which he lay, the clinging wetness of trousers that were soaked with water from the spring, and a bump on his forehead that was throbbing like Indian war drums. He feared that his problems would begin when he tried to stand up, and went very gingerly about it, but came erect without any real difficulty and stood bracing himself off stone with an outstretched right hand.

With the smell of the extinguished candle in his nose, Sam felt instinctively for another match, but realized almost at once that the water with which his pants were drenched had ruined the sulphur tips on those which he had left. Thus, being blind for all practical purposes, he would just have to move around as best he could; and, basing his orientation on what he had known of the cave and the position in which he had fallen, he began groping towards the point at which he believed the entrance to the cave was situated; but he had covered only a yard or two when his feet encountered the edge of a carpet of rubble and fragments turned under his soles, bringing him down painfully on his hands and knees. Cursing again, he picked himself up once more and began wobbling around on the unstable materials that lay unseen beneath his feet, his reaching hands now making contact with the steeply slanting face of the debris that was now piled where he thought the exit had previously been.

For a minute or two he pushed and pulled at the heaped rubble—coughing and choking as he stirred up dust everywhere—but there was neither sufficient strength in his hands nor design in his imagination to achieve much, and he finally sank into a sitting position and let his chin droop into his hands, for he felt weak and dispirited—yes, and defeated too.

But it was not long before a worthwhile reaction set in. Amidst his dejection anger was born. The emotion grew and grew, turning his brain to scarlet, and the power returned to his limbs and the iron to his will. What kind of vermin had done this to him? Men of this western land did not creep up on their fellows and bury them alive with explosions. Sure, they killed, and often and some of them were utterly steeped in evil—but their sins were those of natural minds and scorned the alien wickedness which was so much a part of Bebbinger's criminal ways.

The air was clearing somewhat. Sam got to his feet again, thanking God that he was a miner and used to the darkness. He could stand being buried alive, and would calmly do all that a man could to dig himself out, while drawing strength from the promise to himself that he would survive and exact payment from the man who had done this to him. Concentrating, as he had not done before, he felt around him with hands that were slow and sensitive; and, though he could not be certain as to what was front, back, or sideways in terms of the cave's original shape, he did soon ascertain that the spring as such had disappeared—despite the water still around in places—and that the over-all space in which he was entombed was a good deal smaller than the size of the cavern before the explosion. But that in itself did not worry him, since he was not closely hemmed, and his main concern was for the amount of air that he had left to breathe. He could go without food for days on end, and water for a long time, but no man could live without air for more than a minute or two. The moment his air supply gave out, he would begin to die and all other considerations would cease to matter. Thus, his first task was to try to locate and preserve any air that was coming in through the rockfall and, if none were present, to attempt to create a supply; but, all this was in his mind's eye and, only too aware of the smothering reality of the slipping earth, he feared that what he envisaged might prove utterly beyond the ability of a man without tools to accomplish.

After pausing a moment in a new calculation as to his bearings, Sam applied himself once more to the area in which he believed the entrance to have been originally situated, for something of the aperture might still exist behind the rubble and it would obviously be much easier to bring in oxygen at a spot where the debris could be moved without too much difficulty than to claw away at some point where the opposite could as well be true; but, with all this clear in his mind, getting a start was still a makeshift business and, after a minute or so of tentative fumblings, there was a hint of desperation about the pull that he gave a slab of jutting stone which seemed to be holding up a large amount of other rubble, and down came a fall of rock which might have trapped him completely had he not jumped backwards and tripped into a sitting position on a shape that was unexpectedly soft—the corpse, in fact, of cousin Charlie.

Realizing what had happened, Sam was up again in a fraction of the time that it had taken him to fall—his hair standing on end and a sudden unholy fear of the dead in him—but he shook off this eerie sensation within seconds; for, high up in front of him, as through a thinning mist, he made out a smudge of light and knew that he was no longer totally shut in, as the fall had clearly done of itself what he had been hoping to do by hand and cleared a tiny part of the original cavemouth.

His relief bordering on elation, Sam was tempted to throw himself upon the bank of debris bfore him and try to scramble up to the little opening, but he promptly controlled himself as he realized that any precipitate movement of that kind might cause rubble to roll down from still higher up the pile and fill in the hole once more—perhaps to the extent that he would not be able to open it again and would have lost the supply of air that he had been seeking—yet he simply could not back off in a cowardly manner and squat down beside Charlie Anstey's remains, since to do that would be to die in here for certain, as it was unlikely that anybody would visit this spot again in months or even years.

There was really no choice. It was another case of do or bust. Nor would further delay help anything. So Sam flattened himself on the steep face of the debris and began slowly writhing upwards—his movements mingling those of crab and spider—and, as he kept slipping backwards on the loose rubble and losing many of the inches he had gained, the very thing that he had feared occurred; for, following the displacement of stone on the lower level, that on the higher rattled down into the chink below and instantly cut off the light.

Sam checked in dismay, but was far from ready to cease climbing. No great amount of debris had packed into the aperture, and he was fairly confident that, if he could once reach the spot where it had been, the blockage could be cleared; so he resumed writhing forward and upwards and at last neared the spot, reaching out with his right hand and discovering that he could still feel a faint tremor of air indrawing at the place where the hole had recently been visible. Despite his fears, the signs were good. The barrier between him and the bay beyond the cave could not be an insuperable one, and the amount of debris lying at the top of the pile did not seem large enough to create too many problems of the ongoing kind.

Maintaining the utmost care, Sam swarmed a foot higher on the piled blast fragments and then began removing bits and pieces from the stopped up aperture with first his left hand and then his right. He cast the debris to the rear and away from him with enough force to carry it into the back of the cave before dropping to the floor. He kept up this method of excavation and disposal for a few minutes, and the daylight reappeared in front of him. Now, peering closely, he saw that the worst was behind him, for the ceiling of the aperture was solid rock and the amount of rubble gathered under the roof itself was not fully visible as the chamfering at the top of the blast pile and unlikely to move unless deliberately dug out and set rolling.

Sweating profusely, Sam laboured without

pause, trying to make an orifice through which he could crawl out of the cave head foremost, but the rocks under his elbows were too tightly packed to permit this and he found that the only progress he could make was of the lateral sort. This obviously being the inevitable, he pursued it with no decrease of energy and eventually opened up a slit that followed the terminal line of the explosion's influence upwards and that of the rubble near the top of the sloping pile that was loose enough to come away in his hands, and after what might have been two hours' work or a good deal longer—and ended in his wriggling each extra piece of rock out of the base of the slit by main force—he believed that he had created gap enough to accept his body and eased his feet into the end of it on his right and his head into that on his left, shrugging, twisting, and contorting thereafter until he literally fell through the front wall of the cave and thudded to rest close to where the entrance to the place had once been and an overspill of shattered stone now lay.

Rising, Sam propped himself against the rock to his rear and examined the worst of his cuts and bruises, not to mention his sore fingertips. He was free—able to walk in the daylight again—yet he felt too worn to get excited about it. Everything seemed out of drawing again as he lurched away from his support and staggered to where a horse lay dead on the left of the bay, its legs doubled almost playfully in the air as what was left of it balanced on its back. So Charlie's mount had gone west. The poor brute had been too faithful for its own good. But the state of the dead horse set him thinking about his own. It had undoubtedly been within range of the explosion and, could have been struck by flying rock splinters. The canopy of manzanita—what was left of it—could not have provided much of a shield. On the other hand, the man who had touched off the explosion could have led it to safety before the detonation had occurred. But it was unlikely that the fellow would have bothered about that. His one aim must have been to get to the mouth of the cave, light the fuse to his earlier hidden dynamite, and get away again as quickly as possible. Better go and see how matters stood out there. He wasn't going to further his revenge plans without a horse.

He pushed out through the blasted vegetation ahead of him and, squinting painfully in the fiery brilliance of the sunlight, looked around for his mount—praying that the animal was still alive and wandering somewhere nearby —but it was nowhere in sight and he accepted its loss by sinking down on top of the nearest flat-topped boulder that would make a seat and staring glumly into distances that were beginning to dull faintly in what could only be the changing light of the afternoon. He asked himself whether he ought to walk back to Hazewater immediately, and there make some arrangement about another horse—as well as visit aunt Kathy and explain what had happened out here as it concerned her son's mortal remains—or whether perhaps he ought first to seek the tracks of the man who had dynamited the cavemouth and give himself at least the start of a hunt for his enemies once he had got himself organised again.

It was a matter of choice, he supposed; there was really no better or worse way of doing it, with stable weather conditions in this country that would often leave trace evident for days. When he got down to it, he realized that he had a mind to immediate tracking only because he wished to avoid looking into aunt Kathy's eyes again and reading there her reproaches; for, sensibly speaking, her son's body should be left where it was, since clearing the way to it would represent a good deal of expense and many hours of work for a gang of diggers.

Clapping his hands on his thighs, Sam rose again. It would have to be Hazewater, he guessed; for, in the present circumstances, duty and need suddenly seemed to be in line; but then, from the corner of his left eye, he glimpsed a tiny movement far across the land and raised a hand to shield his sight. He peered intently, then felt a smile coming to his face, for what he could see yonder was a riderless horse—his own for a near certainty—and he supposed the mount must have survived the big bang and simply bolted from the place where it stood, running itself out after a mile or two and then calming down.

This changed matters again. The hunt was on. Dredging up new energy, Sam began plodding down the shallow gradient before him. He headed to the northwest and, at the end of a tramp that semed at least ten times the length it was in fact, he reached the bed of shale on which the horse was standing. The mount was indeed his own, and a quick examination showed that it was uninjured and that nothing on its back had been touched. The animal seemed as pleased to see him as he was to see it, and they held a form of dialogue while he took the waterbottle from his saddle and slaked his thirst. Then, with the container looped back in place, Sam beat the worst of the dust out of his garments and mounted up, guiding his horse back in the direction from which he had come, though he swung eastwards while still some distance short of the cave's position and then back into the north, quartering after that as he sought the tracks of the man—or men— who had tried to bury him alive earlier in the day.

He had expected his task to be an easy one, but oddly enough he lit on no sign anywhere in the neighbourhood, and was beginning to wonder whether his enemies had both come and gone by the trail on the ridge to the south of him, when his eye was again caught by a hovering vulture. He imagined the bird could be the same ill-omened croaker that had cast its shadow on him that morning, and turned his gaze across the fairly distant places over which it was floating, asking himself whether perhaps it had seen something that his own eyes had so far missed, and then he glimpsed what it was shadowing—a rider on a horse who had a burro in tow.

Miner? Could be. There were still plenty of them around, and you could reach the Lode Valley diggings by a trail which ran that way. He felt drawn to the individual yonder, though whoever it was probably held no interest for him whatsoever. And yet even across a gap of three or four miles, it seemed to him now, there was something familiar about the rider. Then, confessing to himself that he was rather at a loose end, Sam gave his horse a slap on the flank and said a trifle reluctantly: 'Come on, horse. Let's go and take a pasear.'

After his initial canter to reduce the gap somewhat, Sam slowed his mount to little better than walking pace and was content just to keep the other rider clearly in sight. Yet all the time he was slightly bothered about whatever it was in the other person that was so familiar. Then, as the figure before him topped a low rise, he felt an instant of startled revelation, for the set of the other's head and shoulders gave her away.

Of course, Lucinda. He had simply not expected to see a female rider in this wilderness of rock and sand. But what the devil was Lucinda doing out here? Had she taken mortal offence at her papa's treatment of her a couple of nights ago and decided to leave home? That would explain the animal at her back which was apparently loaded with supplies. But, no. Aside from the fact that Lucinda hadn't the guts to draw stakes and go it alone, he knew what the answer must be; for he recalled those supplies that Bray Bebbinger had needed and spoken of the night before last in the Valley of the Ravens. It was a fair bet that, for one reason or another, he had not been able to get them in Hazewater by night and had given Lucinda

166

the job of bringing them to him at whatever place he was now hiding out.

Grinning, Sam nodded to himself. It was the luck factor again. Assuming he *had* made no mistake, he needed only to go on following Lucinda and she would bring him to the spot where his enemies were. Perhaps this day was not going to turn out so badly after all.

He flipped a salute skywards, adding ironically. 'Thank you, Mr Vulture!'

CHAPTER TEN

Realizing that there was now good reason not to be spotted by the woman ahead of him, Sam began using the land to conceal his presence as he had not before and letting the gap between him and cousin Lucinda widen perceptibly once more. He kept pursuing in this fashion for the next hour or so, increasingly confident in mind that he could name the girl's destination, for west of them—and she had recently turned due west with the trail that she was following—was a considerable hill of conical shape whose slopes had a thin covering of very large pine trees and whose summit was surmounted by the ruins of the old Spanish Mission of Juan Coronado y Cibola, which was said to have fallen into disuse about forty years ago, when a waggon train of settlers from Europe had brought a particularly virulent strain of smallpox to the village of Juan Coronado—which had been situated at the southern foot of the hill—and shared the disease so generously with both the inhabitants of the

Mission and the village that all had died and those who had perished last still lay unburied. The peasants for a hundred miles around were ever ready to declare Juan Coronado an accursed place, and nobody went there—Spanish or English-speaking—which would obviously suit Bebbinger and friends very well, since they had demonstrated from their quartz mill hideout that they liked to keep a roof over their heads.

Sam relaxed as much as he could. He went on following the girl in his most crafty and patient manner, and saw her arrive under the hill of Juan Coronado in the flat glare of the late afternoon. Pausing on a bank that was overshadowed by a great wedge of jutting rock, Sam watched Lucinda climb the hill and vanish amidst the thickest of the timber towards its top—trees which also obscured the ruins of the Mission and revealed only an odd corner of masonry through their mass.

Considering the likely development of events, Sam reckoned that Lucinda, her job done, would be returning presently over the ground before him—since it was unlikely that she would wish to try to explain a full night away from home to her parents—and he decided that he would leave the immediate section of trail that she would need to retrace and circle out to the north, riding in at the back of the hill and then ascending where he had heard that the slopes were steepest and there was no established path to guide anybody to the ruins on the summit.

Resuming his ride, Sam moved to the right in accordance with his plan and then swung back to approach the northern face of the hill about twenty minutes later. Holding back on his reins, he gazed up at the frowning mass ahead, and then, reaching the foot of the ascent, dismounted, knowing that he and his horse would make less noise on the climb if he led the creature towards the hilltop; so, gripping his mount near the bit, he bent his body to the upward course and drew the horse after him, the sweat once more streaming down his face as he entered the shadows of the mighty cedars near the summit and found himself amidst clouds of dancing gnats.

Beating the insects away from him, Sam slowed for a moment, the muscles of his legs and hips aching; but he saw that one more effort was needed to get him and his mount to the top, and he made it. Walking on the summit now, and still among trees, he realized that he had no more idea of the actual geography of this high place than he had had previously. He kept moving cautiously ahead, eyes darting this way and that as he wondered when the remains of the Mission would come into sight; but suddenly—and unexpectedly—he perceived that the summit was effectively divided into two by an irregular mound that ran across it from east to west, and that the ruins stood forward of the elevated ground and on the southern half of the hill-top.

Out of the big trees, Sam used the bush cover present to approach the central embankment and then climb it, fetching his horse into the gap between two of the burberrry bushes on the raised earth and tying it there. Then, veiled by festooning leaf, he gazed out upon the adobe ruins of the Mission building, with their cruciform windows, dense patches of clinging vines, caved in sections of red-tiled roofing, and bell-tower that still held its rusty bell aloft. The years had not been kind to the place, but parts of it had plainly remained wind and watertight, and Sam had no doubt that Bebbinger and company had often holed up in worse ruins.

Conscious that he might soon encounter the outlaws, Sam drew his revolver which, to his shame, was still in need of a reload from yesterday's fighting, and tipped out its fired shells, replacing them with new ones. Then, holstering the weapon again, he forced out through the light branches before him and moved down the southern face of the mound at a checked run, letting the impetus carry him onto the strip of grass beyond and towards the Mission's back wall.

He saw a black wooden door near the building's western end and, turning right, headed for it. The door looked as if it might be the way into a vestry or some other small room. Anyway, he had made up his mind that he would enter the Mission through it—providing that it was not locked—and thus, perhaps, avoid the period of exposure to any watching eyes that walking round to the front door on the other side of the place might bring.

Sam reached the door, and saw that its latch was connected to a circle of iron. Gripping the ring, he turned it to the right and pushed inwards, the door offering no resistance but opening with a loud creaking noise, and he slipped between the jamb and woodwork and found himself in just such a small room as he had expected. There was a cot set against the wall on his right, while ahead of him, between the cot and the wall on his left, was a narrow walkway which led to another door that was placed in the rear wall of the little room.

Darting along the narrow strip of floor before him, Sam came to the inner door. Here, with his hand upon the latch, he glanced back and saw now that the cot was occupied and that the stories told of Juan Coronado's unburied dead were true; for there, shrunken within a rusty black cassock and grinning a mummy's grin, lay the remains of a man who had apparently died in the prime of his years, for the hair that still clung to the brownish skin of his skull was a silky black and the teeth in his horrible grin were flawless and only lightly tinged with the yellow of the years. Shuddering, Sam turned his back on this long dead and undoubtedly once venerable priest, restoring his attention to the door in front of him, and he lifted the latch and drew inwards, the hinges here creaking less noisily than those opposite and the door opening onto what was clearly the western end of the Mission's chapel, for a font and crumbling pews were visible on the cracked mosaics of the floor.

Sam stepped forward a pace. He peeped round the side of the doorway and peered to his left. He found himself gazing down the length of the chapel, which ended in an upturned altar, piles of broken glass, and a more general ruin that included great beams from the collapsed roof at that end of the building and heaps of bricks and plaster from the walls. Apart from himself, the building seemed to be deserted by the living at present, but he could hear male voices in conversation outside the main door of the Mission, which was situated more or less in the centre of the wall opposite and still had a touch of carved grandeur about it.

Leaving the side room, Sam tip-toed out into the body of the chapel, skirting the pews directly in his path and following the aisles round until he reached the main door. Here he paused again; then, edging up to the gap that had been created when the twin leaves of the door had been set at angles of forty-five degrees to each other, he looked through the porch beyond and out onto the ground at the front of the Mission, where he saw Bray Bebbinger and another man standing on the right—arms folded and heads nodding sagely—as they watched Lucinda Anstey's still just visible figure descending the path that led down the eastern face of Mission hill and away into the shadowy badlands that extended for most of the eighteen or twenty miles that lay between Juan Coronado and the town of Hazewater.

More engrossed than was perhaps wise, Sam was startled about then by a faint sound at his back. Aware that it had been the suddenly careless footfall of a man who was creeping up on him, Sam whirled round from left to right and, reacting to the presence of a face momentarily glimpsed, whipped out his gun and struck with its barrel, the steel catching the outlaw who had been bent on surprising him a heavy though glancing blow on the left side of the skull. The outlaw unhinged instantly, and fell with a thud, then lay unstirring.

Judging that the man's fall must have been heard outside, Sam spun round again and sprang to the front of the porch beyond the main door, covering Bebbinger and his black-jowled, broken-nosed companion as they swung to face him, their hands moving toward their revolvers. 'Hold it!' Sam warned, thumbing back the hammer of his weapon. 'Unbuckle your gunbelts and throw them as far away from you as you can. damn you, Bebbinger—careful! I'd as lief blast a hole in your belly as take you in to the sheriff. My duty as a good citizen demands that I do this right—unless you give me the excuse to do it wrong. What d'you say?'

'Seems like you've got the drop on us for now,' Bray Bebbinger conceded, his gunbelt already hanging from his left hand and his eyebrow on that side lifted. 'How many lives have you got, Cade?'

'Miaaouw!' Sam acknowledged. 'Throw it!'

Bebbinger cast his gunbelt away from him, and his companion did the same, both belts fall-ing closer on the right of the men than Sam would have preferred, but too far away never-theless for there to be any chance of the pistols being instantly recovered.

'Weaklings!' Sam jeered. 'Now where's that gold of mine?'

'What have you done to Ike Crossman?' Beb-binger countered.

'Half-brained him,' Sam replied dismissive-ly. 'It should teach him not to sneak up on folks. Oh, I get what happened now, Bebb-inger! You boys must have been watching for Lucinda, and seen me drawing along behind her. I ought to have considered that. Black mark, Sam boy! You guys stand high here, and can see much. It was a nice little trap you laid for me, but it didn't quite work as you meant. Now—where's my gold?'

'At the foot of the bell-tower,' Bebbinger replied, 'and your mules are cropping the grass at the western end of the Mission.'

'Sorry,' Sam said. 'I'm not going to be fool enough to look that way.'

'Maybe you should look round more often,' the gang boss remarked with a sneer. 'You were easy meat when I touched off that dyna-mite. Deaf as a post!'

'Maybe,' Sam admitted. 'But I'm still here.'

'Ain't he mean and nasty,' the second outlaw observed.

'No pedigree, Reed,' Bebbinger sniffed. 'How are you going to handle the two of us, Cade?'

Sam did not allow his expression to alter by so much as a twitch. But it was a problem all the same. The pair must be bound. If he left their hands and feet free, sooner or later they were going to get up to mischief. Yet all alone like this, how was he to get the ropes on them? It appeared that he would have to become as mean and nasty as the man named Reed had lately suggested that he was, and knock them unconscious with the barrel of his Colt. But every time you hit a man like that you took the risk of fracturing his skull, though he imagined that Bebbinger and Reed had bone enough up there to resist any lasting harm. Anyhow, he was going to hit them, and to hell with the rest. 'Turn yourselves round!' he ordered.

'He's got the idea, Horace,' Bebbinger said wryly. 'He might learn something yet.'

'Heck!' Reed muttered.

'I don't aim to keep repeatin' myself,' Sam gritted. 'Just face about.'

Then, from the left of where he stood, he heard the voice of Lucinda Anstey call: 'Drop your gun, Sam! I'm holding a rifle on you, and I'll be happy to shoot if you force me to it!'

Sam threw a rapid glance towards the southern edge of the hill's summit, and saw that Lucinda had risen off the slope on that side. A cocked Winchester was drawn in firmly against her right shoulder, and there was no shake in the weapon as her finger whitened on the trigger. Sam could have called her something unmentionable, and wondered what her mother would think of her now. For here she was prepared to do real harm. Plainly, for this reason or that, she had doubled back on the path leading down the eastern side of the hill—spotted what was happening near the Mission door—and then crept round the hilltop to the position from which she was threatening him now. 'You disappoint me, Lucinda,' he now commented rather weakly. 'I used to believe that blood was thicker than water.'

'So now you know better!' the girl pouted. 'My brother and Issy Kaufmann are dead because of you. And there was what you did to me that day!'

'Are you *still* on about that?' Sam asked disgustedly.

'What have you been doing, Sam?' Bebbinger tut-tutted. 'She's going to kill you all right if you don't drop that six-shooter.'

Sam let the Colt fall at his feet. When would fortune stay on his side? But then he heard a movement at his back. Craning, he saw that

Crossman—the man whom he'd recently flattened with his revolver barrel—was up again and lurching towards him, Colt in hand and face full of a glassy-eyed confusion. The gun went off, its explosion racketing through the ruined Mission, and Sam felt the slug burn through the slack of his shirt and rush onwards.

Lucinda, directly in line with the pistol's flash, uttered a terrible scream and dropped her rifle, staring down at the wound in her chest from which the blood had begun pumping redly. Then she sank to her knees, sobbing piteously, and suddenly pitched forward onto her face, the ugly twitching of her limbs telling that she had just died.

Everybody had been momentarily rooted by the shock of what had occurred—Sam no less than the rest—but now, alert to the need, he was the first to recover and, bending rapidly, snatched up his sixgun from where it was lying and screwed round, firing upwards from knee-level into Crossman's chest as the badman shot at him a second time. Again Crossman missed by the smallest of margins, but Sam's bullet went where it mattered, and the outlaw fell lifelessly and spun, his face coming to rest against the eastern wall of the porch.

Facing about once more, his mouth open to warn Bebbinger and Reed anew, Sam was met by a kick in the pit of the stomach that the gang boss delivered with some force. Hurt, Sam staggered backwards, but held on to both his wits and his pistol; and, as he perceived that Bebbinger was about to dive at him in an attempt to take the legs from under him, he brought his Colt back into line and triggered off, his bullet raking the boss outlaw's lower left ribs and burning open his shirt so that the bloody groove of the surface wound was visible beneath.

Checked, Bebbinger did a peculiar dance on the spot; then, forgetting all about the dive that he had essayed, sprang abruptly to his left and thereafter whirled to face southwards and began loping towards the gunbelt that he had been made to throw aside.

Thumbing at his hammer, Sam followed Bebbinger's movements with the muzzle of his revolver, determined to hold his fire until the instant that he was sure of a solid hit; and therein was his mistake, for Reed had not delayed to find out how successful his boss's attack on Sam was going to prove, but had started running for his gunbelt at the moment that he had seen the staggering Cade turn all his attention to Bebbinger.

Now, having reached his gunbelt and plucked his Colt out of its holster, Reed pointed his weapon at Sam—who was still concentrating elsewhere—and began to fan the hammer, getting off five shots in less than two seconds; but the shooting was too fast for any real accuracy, and the only hurts that Sam received from the hail of lead were a nick above his left elbow and something similar on the inside of his right leg just above the knee.

Cursing the emptiness of his sixgun, Reed attempted to fumble a partial reload, but he had received all the opportunity that Cade was prepared to give him, and Sam drew himself erect now and shifted his aim to the black-chinned man, firing off an extended arm and hitting the outlaw in the forehead. Reed fell onto his back, limbs slack and unnaturally twisted, and it was obvious that he would never rise again.

There was a sharp detonation on Sam's left, and a slug hummed past his ear on the same side. Glancing round, as he again squeezed back his hammer, Sam perceived that Bebbinger had recovered his pistol almost faster than seemed possible and had just opened fire on him. Turning enough to meet the gang boss eye-to-eye, Sam fired as Bebbinger once more blasted at him, and he saw the tall outlaw wince and lift a tremulous foot in the same split second as he was himself aware of hot lead burning through the wedge of thick muscle behind his left armpit.

Sam felt a lot of his stength drain away, and his will seemed to falter. That bullet had really told. But he forced his gun back on target and got off another shot before his enemy could do the same. Bebbinger staggered, firing into the ground, and this time looked startled; then, seeming to lose his courage—or to decide that discretion was the better part of valour—he threw himself into a run, making for the southern edge of the summit and, reaching it, sprang into the shelter of the hillside below before turning right and racing westwards, the top of his head just visible to the still aggressive Sam, who fired a final shot at it and then stood watching as the gang boss reappeared on the summit itself at a spot about eighty yards away, where three horses were cropping—obviously the mounts which had carried the outlaw trio to this place—grabbed a big dun stallion, mounted up, and went spurring off the hilltop, moving down through the trees on the slope beyond in a southwesterly direction.

Conscious that he must now conserve his strength, Sam resisted the sudden temptation to go pelting around the end of the ruined Mission on his right with the idea of reaching his horse as fast as possible and immediately starting a chase. He had a strong feeling that there was no need for haste. Sam was confident that, despite the man's display of energy when leaving this spot, those last two bullets had hurt Bebbinger badly and the gang boss would not be going too far. So he stood and reloaded his Colt, then holstered the weapon before setting off round the western end of the Mission and making for the mound on top of which he had tethered his horse.

Locating the animal, he freed it from the burberry bush to which it was tied and then led it down the front of the raised ground, mounting up on the strip of level grass behind the Mission. Then, ignoring the blood which was flowing down his left side and soaking the seat of his pants, he kicked his horse into motion and steered it round the western end of the building adjacent, riding across the forward half of the hilltop after that and then entering the trees which shaded the same southwesterly course that the gang boss had used while fleeing from the summit.

He descended the hill at a measured pace, glimpsing, on the plain below and to his left, the adobe ruins of the long defunct village named after the Coronado Mission above. Then, at the foot of the hill, he moved onto a considerable field of red sand, and here the tracks left by Bebbinger's horse were so clear that a blind man might have picked them out. Settling on the tracks, Sam brought his horse to full gallop, preparing to ride into what was now the evening light for as long as it took. They soon came to a trail of sorts and drubbed along it through the still air, the horse lathering in the heat which radiated from the land. The miles began to add up, but presently Sam saw Bebbinger on the way ahead. The outlaw had obviously pushed his mount too hard from the very beginning and the creature was now starting to flag. As the shadows lengthened and merged upon the desert scene, Bebbinger's lead grew smaller and smaller, and before long it was reduced to less than a quarter of a mile. Then, at no great distance ahead, Sam made out a long climb into places where the Sierra Nevada was turning black against the scarlet glow of the setting sun. He knew that this was the end of it, for Bebbinger's horse would never manage even part of the climb, and its rider must already be aware of it.

Then, as if this were just another ride and he had had enough of it, Bebbinger pulled up and dismounted at the southern edge of the trail. After that, making a crepe-like silhouette in the fiery reflection from the west, he crossed the beaten track and lowered himself into a sitting position on a flat-topped boulder. Now he drew his Colt and, setting the hammer at half-cock and opening the loading gate, spun out the fired shells from his cylinder in preparation for a reload.

Slowing his horse to a trot, Sam approached the outlaw in the full confidence that, at this extremity, Bebbinger would attempt nothing underhand. As the gap between them narrowed their eyes met, and Sam answered his enemy's cold smile with a curt nod. Then he stopped his mount about eight yards short of Bebbinger's seat and cocked a leg, lowering himself slowly to the ground. 'Hell of a place we've got for it,' he observed conversationally, moving a pace or two closer to the gang boss and then halting again.

'It's a poor place to die,' Bebbinger agreed, feeding shells into his revolver with fingers that had a tremble of weakness about them. 'One— or both.'

'You're booked, Bray,' Sam observed, studying the positions of the two bullet wounds in the outlaw's upper body. 'I figured those slugs of mine hit you hard.'

Bebbinger shrugged. 'You were lucky back there at the Mission, Sam, but this is where your luck runs out.'

'We'll see.'

'I'm a top gun, and you're a miner.'

'Correction. You're a dying man, mister, but I'm still mostly whole.'

'That's how you see it, eh?' Bebbinger mused, closing the gate on his reload and thumbing the hammer of his gun all the way back.

Sam gripped the butt of his holstered pistol. 'Put it away.'

'Don't reckon I'm up to that,' Bebbinger said feebly. 'How fast can you draw it, Sam?'

Sam saw the muzzle of the other's gun begin rising. He snatched his revolver out of leather and got off his first shot a particle of time ahead of the weapon opposite flashing at him. Then it was blast and counter-blast, with gunsmoke pulsing black rings in the motionless air, while the echoes of the shots cracked and rolled around the desert. Eyes slitted and left hand clenched, Sam stood upright through the exchange, feeling the wind of one slug on the right side of his neck and the breath of another on his left temple. But, as Bebbinger's gun fell silent, he knew himself no worse hurt than before, while the gang boss lay as he had that moment fallen off his seat, head and shoulders on the ground behind the rock and feet pointed into the air off stiffened legs. Sam gave the feet a shove, and the body twisted aside and flattened at the rear of the boulder. It was all over; and the last and furthest echoes of the shooting growled into silence against the mountains of the west.

Holstering his gun, Sam lifted a hand to his head. He was feeling kind of swimmy. It must be the loss of blood, for he was still bleeding down his left side. Heck, now—he'd bet himself five dollars he wasn't going to make it back to Hazewater. Nor yet halfway. Wasn't that how things went? Having come through a shoot-out with a top gun, he was going to fall off his horse in the middle of nowhere and die. It wasn't fitting; and, what was worse, it was a waste of effort.

But then he remembered the Lode Valley was over to his right and not more than two miles away. He had friends in Lode Valley. There he would find Ralph Figgins, and Ralph's straw-haired daughter, the shapely Harry. He had told the pair that he would visit them. Well, it was a bit early for that, socially speaking, and also a mite late in the day, but he felt sure that Harry and her papa would soon understand how it was with him and make allowances.

He managed to turn round; then staggered back to his horse. He clambered into his saddle —a task that seemed tougher than climbing

Mount Grant—and, for his fourth and almost impossible trick, contrived to point his horse in the right direction and hang on to its mane as he kneed it into motion. After that it was just a matter of sticking with it until the walls of Lode Valley reared into the gloom on either hand and a voice which could only belong to Ralph Figgins warned him to 'stop right where he was and give an account of himself.'

'Sam Cade,' he croaked in response. 'Here visitin'.'

'Sam?' blonde Harry's voice inquired from nearby. 'Sam?'

'Yeah, Sam,' he agreed, making out the girl's hazy figure standing a few yards to his right.

'We heard shooting a while ago,' Figgins informed him. 'Did that have anything to do with you?'

'I was part of it,' Sam admitted.

'Figures.'

'Don't sound so damned disapproving,' Sam complained. 'Harry.'

'Yes, Sam?'

'Come here.'

The girl advanced until she stood beside his horse. 'You're hurt!' she cried. 'There's blood everywhere!'

'Hush up!' he advised. 'Are you strong?'

'I am.'

188

'Good—'cos I've got a feeling I'm about to fall off this danged hoss.'

'Sam!'

'There she goes again,' he muttered, and took his tumble, a darkness deeper than the night claiming him.

CHAPTER ELEVEN

Sam was feeling much more like himself now.
He had lain in the Figgin's tent for the last
four days, and had been a very sick man; but
now his wounds were on the mend, and Miss
Figgins had put the blood back into his de-
pleted veins with a liberal supply of venison
broth. In fact Sam was feeling so much more
like himself this afternoon that he had not
been able to help noticing that blonde Harry
was not only beautiful but all woman too.
Indeed he had just had his right hand slapped
hard and been splashed with cold water to
discourage him from being so enthusiastic
about the aspects of her physique that pleased
him. 'I do declare!' Harry exclaimed indig-
nantly. 'If I couldn't see otherwise, I'd say
you had four pair of hands. You should be
locked up for the safety of poor motherless
girls!'

'But I only wanted to kiss you!' Sam protested.

'There are kisses and kisses,' the blonde

retorted, more worldly wise than the invalid had expected. 'Yours are the sort that should be avoided—unless a girl is prepared to take the consequences.'

'You're not?' he wheedled.

'What would my papa say?' Harry wondered, turning her eyes to heaven. 'And him out on your business, Sam Cade.'

'Yeah,' Sam admitted, 'I guess I've been a nuisance at that. What with your pa having to pack all those bodies into Hazewater and then explain to my uncle Bert and aunt Kathy how their daughter died and their son's body is maybe better left where it's lying. Now he's out fetchin' that gold of mine from the Mission of Juan Coronado. I'll surely be glad to see him back here—even if his presence does kinda cramp my style around his lovely daughter.'

'You've got a fox's eye,' Harry said severely. 'You are wicked, Sam Cade!'

'Isn't it better you should find out before we're married?' Sam asked complacently.

'Have some broth.'

'Got any whisky?'

'Not for you,' she answered. 'You're a sight too frisky already. I dread to think what might happen if you got a cup of papa's moonshine inside you.'

'I could make you real happy,' he assured

191

her, tongue in cheek; for he had an idea that she didn't really think his wickedness was such a bad thing at all.

Her frown was forbidding, but there was no mistaking the twinkle in her eye; and then she looked sharply to her left and put a finger to her lips. 'Ssssh! I think pa has just got back.'

Then Sam heard the sounds too—the click of a riding horse's shoes and the braying of a mule—and a few moments later Harry was confirmed in her belief that her father had returned, for Ralph Figgins thrust his head in at the tent doorway and said: 'It was all there, Cade. Everything was just like you said.'

'Good,' Sam acknowledged. 'That's just fine.'

'Never saw such ore,' Figgins confessed. 'I've been sick with envy all the way home. There's enough gold in that stuff to make you rich as Creosote.'

'Should keep me in the necessaries,' Sam agreed.

'I could steal it off you,' Figgins growled.

'Tell you what,' Sam said munificently. 'You can have the gold, and I'll have the girl.'

'You!' cried the outraged blonde, slapping him round the ear.

Aware that he had deserved it, Sam grinned

ruefully at Figgins and rubbed the smarting lobe.

'You ought to be over the moon, boy,' the big miner said, continuing to view the invalid rather sourly.

'I am,' Sam responded, 'but not about that. I'll tell you the truth about gold, Mr Figgins. The fun's in seeking it, and the misery's in trying to keep it.'

'Your gold is like that?' Figgins asked in amazement.

'Cade's gold is no different from the rest,' Sam replied, suddenly grave; and then he reached out and took the hand with which the girl had slapped him.

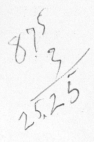

Magna Print Books hope you have enjoyed this Large Print book. All our Large Print titles are designed for the easiest reading, and all our books are made to last. Other Magna Large Print Books are available at your library, through selected book-stores, or direct from the publisher. For more information about our current and forth-coming Large Print titles, please send your name and address to:

Magna Print Books
Magna House, Long Preston,
Nr Skipton, North Yorkshire,
England. BD23 4ND.

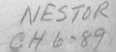